Also by Rick Marchetti

DARK GLASSES and Other Tales
THE RIVER
IRIS
MURDER IN THE VALLEY
THE CABIN IN THE WOODS and Other Tales

187 MUSIC ROW

♪ ♪♪ ♪ ♪♪ ♪

RICK MARCHETTI

Cover Art ©2014 Jennie Finken

This is a work of fiction. Any resemblance to
people, living or dead, is unintentional and entirely
coincidental.

No part of this book may be reproduced or
transmitted in any form or by any means, electronic or
mechanical, including photocopying, recording, or by
any information storage and retrieval system, without
permission in writing from the author.

AUTHOR'S NOTE

For the sake of the story, I have taken certain liberties with locations in and around Nashville. In some instances I've moved things geographically; in others, I've created places (i.e.: Sonny's Place). Also, 187 Music Row is not a physical address; rather, 1-8-7 is Police Code for the crime of murder. Finally –and most importantly- I have no insider knowledge of either the Nashville Police Department or the Medical Examiner's Office, and it should not be inferred that the portrayals herein reflect actual people or events. So far as I know, Forensics is not an offering at Southern Methodist University.

6:03 PM

"Nine-one-one, what's your emergency?"

"He's dead," the man answered, dazed. He couldn't take his eyes off the blood, which had stained Big Jim's white shirt crimson. When he was finally able to look away, he saw that blood had splattered on the wall behind the body. As he watched, one fat, red drop ran down the glass covering one of the pictures there, pooled when it reached the frame, then dropped silently into the plush carpet. In the photo, Jim and Roy Clark, one of his closest friends, went on serenading the crowd at the Ryman Auditorium, totally unaware of what had happened right in front of them.

"Who's dead, sir?"

"My boss. He's dead."

"Where are you calling from, sir?"

"Diamond in the Rough Publishing. On the

corner of Sixteenth and Grand."

"An ambulance is on its way. What is your name, sir?"

The man dropped the phone as if it had burned him, then picked up the receiver and carefully placed it back in the cradle. As he did, he could still hear the operator asking for his name.

ONE

Earlier...

Tires crunched on the gravel driveway in front of a large, upscale house in a suburb of Nashville. A middle-aged, but very well-preserved, blond sat up in bed, eyes wide, the sheet falling away from her perfect, surgically-enhanced breasts. She grabbed at it and covered herself, as if modesty were suddenly important to her.

"Get up," she hissed at the man lying next to her, snoring lightly. She reached out and shook him, and not gently. "Wake up. My husband's home." The man stirred, then his eyes snapped open as he processed what she had just said.

"Shit," he breathed, rolling off the bed.

"Hurry up," she urged as a car door slammed. The man gathered up his things frantically, pulled on his boxers and jeans, and bolted from the bedroom, carrying his shoes and shirt. Footsteps clicked on the flagstone walk leading to the front door. The shoeless man went into the kitchen, which was on the back side of the house, and slipped out the back door while the woman made a beeline for the bathroom. As she did, she saw something under the bed. Socks. White. Certainly not her Brooks Brothers husband's. She snatched them up and ran into the bathroom, shaking, and locked the door behind her. Not a moment too soon. She heard the front door open.

One street over, JT Wheeler slid behind the wheel of his pick-up truck. He had bought the truck just before leaving Rhode Island, where he had been born and raised, because he thought –mistakenly, it turned out– that it would make him seem more "authentic" to the other songwriters in Nashville. Once he got there, however, he quickly learned that all that mattered was the songs he wrote, not what he drove or how he dressed. Vernon Sills, the first 'real' songwriter to accept JT into the Nashville songwriting community, had told him one night over beers at The Broken Spoke Saloon that 'Hats don't write hits', a not-thinly-veiled reference to all the newcomers who descended on the town -"like damned locusts", Vernon said- thinking they were the real deal just because they dressed the part. So, while he didn't wear the unofficial "uniform" – cowboy hat and boots - he had developed a fondness for the truck, so he kept it, despite the fact that it got lousy mileage and didn't always start on the first try. He jammed the key into the ignition and sent up a silent prayer, convinced that the irate husband of his latest conquest would be hot on his heels, most likely brandishing a nine-iron. He needn't have worried; the husband had no idea what had been going on all afternoon in his own bed -although he did make it a point to chastise her for it not being made- and the truck started right up. As he shifted into gear, he suddenly realized he wasn't wearing socks. His eyes grew wide and he slammed his hands on the steering wheel.

"Dammit," he exclaimed, but then began to laugh as the absurdity of the situation sank in. After all, what did he care? An angry husband certainly couldn't trace a pair of sweat socks to their rightful owner, now could he? As for the woman, well, she was just another notch on his well-worn bedpost. Or, in this case, *her* bedpost. Let her husband figure it out. Unless she was foolish enough to offer up JT's name, she would bear the brunt of her cuckolded husband's anger, not him. Still laughing, he eased off the clutch and pulled away.

As he drove home through the tree-lined outskirts of the city, JT's good humor quickly faded. The closer he got to the city proper, the more he thought about why he came to Nashville in the first place. *Certainly not to get drunk and sleep with other men's wives*, he thought. He remembered his teenage years, back in Rhode Island. While all his friends were outside playing sports and, later, fixing cars and chasing girls, he was holed up in his parents' basement, writing songs. His friends teased him about it, but while they were, in his opinion anyway, wasting their time, he knew how he wanted to make his living. After high school, he worked whatever job he could find and saved pretty much every penny he made, preparing for the day he could pack his guitar and some clothes and head to Nashville to find his fortune. His only expenses were notebooks, cassette tapes, and guitar strings. But, since he never thought of himself as an accomplished musician or singer, his songs never made it beyond the basement walls, unknown to everyone but him and his family. He knew he should get out and let people hear what he'd written, but he didn't have the confidence.

One day, while he was driving to his job at a local gas station singing snatches of one of his original songs, he heard a radio ad for a recording studio in Providence that was holding a songwriting contest. First prize was a complete demo tape, studio musicians and all. He spent his shift at the station trying to decide which song he would submit to the contest. Visions of making a demo that he could send to publishers in Nashville filled his head. He knew that, once the movers and shakers in Country music heard his songs, his dream of being a professional songwriter would be in the bag. Even though he didn't have the confidence to perform his songs in public, he did have abundant confidence in the songs themselves. He finally settled on a ballad, a tune called "Just One Night" that he had written about a girl named Sarah. They had met a year or so before when they both worked at a small local restaurant. They had talked all the time and, although he wanted to be much more than friends, he never told her how he felt. Instead, he went home night after night with his secret safely locked away and wrote a dozen songs professing his love for her over the next several months, songs she would never hear. He fantasized constantly about being at work and walking into the kitchen. She would be there, listening to one of his songs on the radio, mesmerized by the beauty of it, lost in the moment. When she saw him, she would ask who he wrote it for, a hopeful note in her voice. In a scene worthy of the big screen, he would confess that it was about her and she would fall into his arms, totally and unconditionally in love. But life isn't a movie, she never heard the songs and, by the time he had finally found the courage to tell her how he felt, Sarah was engaged to a guy she met while taking courses at the local community college. JT moped for awhile, wrote some more songs and, eventually, got back to business as usual.

When he got home after work that night, he didn't even bother to eat or shower; he just announced to his parents that he would be recording –his signal to them to 'keep the noise to a dull roar', as his father liked to joke. He went down to his makeshift studio in the basement and set up the microphones; one aimed toward his acoustic guitar's sound hole, the other inches away from his mouth. He slipped a fresh tape into the cassette deck, checked his tuning, and ran through the song once to make sure he had it down, the guitar was in tune, the levels were right; basically checking for potential problems. Once he was convinced he was ready, he hit RECORD and started strumming the chords to the intro. Just as he began to sing, he heard the shrill of the telephone upstairs coming through his mic and into his headphones. He pushed the STOP button, aggravated.

"Crap," he spat. "Stupid phone." He waited a minute to make sure his mother didn't suddenly open the cellar door and call down that it was for him. Satisfied that wasn't going to happen, he rewound the tape and started again. He strummed, he sang. It sounded great. Halfway through, one of his guitar strings snapped.

"Crap!" he hissed again. "I don't believe this." He opened his guitar case and found a replacement string, took off the broken one, put on the new one. Two minutes later, he was once again ready to record. 'Third time's the charm,' he told himself. And it was. His third take was flawless. The next morning he put the tape, his entry form, and a check for fifteen dollars in a padded envelope, dropped it in the mail box on the corner, and began the waiting game.

TWO

Six weeks later, JT found himself in the studio, the Grand Prize winner in the song contest. He tried to see everything at once, caught up in the hustle and bustle going on around him. His producer, a veteran of the highly-regarded Providence music scene who had once played guitar with a band that made a brief national splash, was a guy named Dale Mitchell. Dale had assembled a team of six musicians and a vocalist who rivaled those you would find in any studio in any music center, and they nailed "Just One Night" in two takes. Then the producer worked his magic, tweaking, mixing, dubbing; getting everything just so. JT had walked into the studio at ten in the morning with a raw song and a dream, and walked out at eleven that same night with a reel of quarter-inch tape and two cassettes. His head was spinning. It was a day –and feeling- he'd never forget. He left the studio with his feet barely making contact with the ground, dying to tell someone. As he sat in his car, he spotted a pay phone and decided to call Sarah, then just as quickly convinced himself that her boyfriend would answer the phone. He didn't think he could handle that. Finally, he drove home, elated and depressed at the same time. When he let himself into the house, his parents had turned in for the night. He had no one to tell about his incredible day in the studio. He undressed and slipped into bed, where he spent a long time staring at the ceiling before finally dropping off to sleep. When he woke the next morning, he briefly wondered if it had all been a dream.

Now, parked in a scenic overlook, he snapped back to the present as he stood next to his truck. He let his eyes wander over the Nashville skyline, wondering how his life –and career- could be unraveling right before his eyes while he just stood by and watched it happen. He had come to town as a complete unknown but, after a few weeks, had met a veteran songwriter named Vernon Sills. Vernon took him under his wing, a lucky break that most never get. Before that, JT had been walking up and down Music Row, knocking on doors.

Before he left Rhode Island, still awash in the glow of the recording session, he thought it would be easy. He would walk into a publisher's office, hand him his tape, and sign a contract to be a staff writer on the spot. He was shocked, then, to find out that it was in no way, shape, or form, that simple. When he approached the publishing companies' offices, the doors were all locked. At each office, he would have to press the entry buzzer and wait. Each and every time, some unseen person, usually a young woman, would politely ask who was there and then, just as politely, turn him away. He endured this for three months. At the time, he had been staying at the Days Inn on Demonbreun Street, just across the interstate from downtown and a short walk from "The Row". Now he realized he would have to move out of the motel and find an apartment. He had some money saved up, but it wasn't going to last forever. He hadn't planned on getting a day job in Nashville, but now that seemed not just possible, but likely. One afternoon, totally discouraged, he had wandered toward downtown, until he found himself in a small coffee and donut shop, the Dip 'n Sip on Broadway. He must have looked completely out of sorts as he nursed his coffee and stared at the back wall of the shop, wondering just what the hell he had gotten himself into, because an older man sitting a few tables away stood up and approached the counter where JT was seated. He dropped onto the stool beside him and sat quietly for a few minutes, sipping his coffee, then finally spoke without looking at him.

"It's a tough town, son," he said in a quiet voice. "You look like someone who found that out today." JT, who, up until that point had been pretty much numb, suddenly felt like crying. It was a combination of feeling foolish for coming to Nashville so obviously unprepared, losing what little confidence he had come with, and realizing that his money would soon run out.

After a time, he glanced at the stranger, who

immediately stuck out his hand and smiled.

"Vernon Sills," he said. "Call me Rusty." JT shook with him. Rusty studied him, nodding. "Yep," he said. "You got the look about you. Came here from East Japeep thinking you were gonna sweep into town and be the second coming of George Strait. Am I right? Of course, I am," he finished, agreeing with himself before JT could respond.

"I'm a writer," JT said in a soft voice, "not a singer."

Rusty nodded. "Uh-huh." He sipped his coffee. "Where do you call home?" he asked companionably.

"Um, I'm staying at the Days Inn," JT said.

Rusty chuckled. "I mean, where are you from?" he asked, his pale blue eyes twinkling in his seamed face. "I came here from San Antone. Back in seventy-two."

"Oh," JT said, feeling foolish. "I'm from Rhode Island."

Rusty's eyes opened wide. "Rhode Island?" he repeated, seemingly taken aback. "That's that island south of New York, right?"

JT shook his head. He had heard this plenty of times, but it always surprised him.

"That's Long Island. Rhode Island is a state."

"Oh. Well, it's still up north. Those folks even know what Country music is up there?"

It was JT's turn to laugh. "Yeah, we know what it is. We've got some great writers and musicians. You should hear my demo. The guys who played and sang on it are awesome."

"Is that so?" Rusty teased. "Well, where's this awesome demo at?" He tilted his head back, challenging, but the friendly smile never left his face. JT was suddenly suspicious. Rusty seemed to read his thoughts. "Now come on, son; nobody's looking to steal your song. Let's hear it."

Slowly JT reached into his shirt pocket and pulled out a cassette tape. He glanced around and shrugged. "How are you going to listen to it here?" he asked.

Rusty tipped him a wink and plucked the tape from his hand. "Watch and learn, son," he said. "Watch and learn." He looked back toward the door leading to the kitchen. "Jessie!" he bellowed. "Jessie, come on out here, darlin'."

The attractive blond waitress who had served JT his coffee popped through the door. "Whatchoo-all yelling 'bout, Rusty?" she asked with an affectionate smile, then rolled her eyes at JT and shook her head. Even in his current state, JT had noticed that smile, and the southern accent that came with it.

Rusty returned the smile. "Would you be so kind as to put this tape, which belongs to my young friend here…" He glanced at JT. "What's your name, son?"

"JT."

"Alrighty, then. JT it is." He turned back to Jessie. "Would you be so kind as to slip JT's tape into that boom box you got sitting back there?" She took the tape from him and bent down, still smiling. When she straightened up, she was holding a huge Sony tape player, which she placed on the counter. She popped the door open and slipped the tape inside. "Thank you, darlin'," Rusty said. "And turn it way up, wouldja?"

JT's eyes got wide. He put a hand on Rusty's arm. "NO!" he whisper-shouted. Then he lowered his voice even more and motioned with his head. "There are people over there." Rusty glanced toward where JT, mouth hanging open, was staring. An older couple was sitting at a booth in the corner and five young women, all wearing shirts from nearby Vanderbilt University, were sitting at two tables they'd pushed together in the middle of the floor.

"So there are," Rusty said, nodding gravely. "'Scuse me, son." He turned away from JT and raised his voice. "Say there, folks. You wouldn't mind hearing a song by an up-and-coming new songwriter, my buddy JT here, would you?" He didn't wait for an answer before he turned to JT, smiled, and said, "See, pardner, they don't mind at all."

JT felt beads of sweat pop out on his face, and he was momentarily dizzy. He covered his face and could feel his heartbeat in his temples.

"Don't," he whispered into his hands, but it was too late. Rusty punched a button on the boom box and the intro to his song filled the little shop. He ducked his head, embarrassed. After about thirty seconds, he couldn't take it anymore and glanced back at the other customers. To his shock, they were all listening raptly. And smiling. There was a light touch on his arm and he turned back toward the counter to see Jessie standing in front of him. She, too, was smiling.

"This is real good, sugar," she said, then walked back toward the kitchen. Three minutes later, with the last strains of the song *–his* song- dying in the air, JT was shocked to realize that each and every one of the strangers was applauding. Rusty sat next to him, nodding and smiling, then his face turned serious, and he leaned in close.

"Don't ever hang your head when people are

listening to your music, son," he said quietly. "If you're embarrassed by what you've written, you've got no business being here. I'm gonna hook you up with my publisher and see what we can do about getting you up and running." JT was too shocked to respond.

Later, when Rusty dropped him off at the Days Inn, JT had asked him, "Why are you doing all this for me? You don't know me from Adam."

Rusty hadn't hesitated before answering. "Because," he explained. "this is how Nashville is. People help one another. When I first got to town, I didn't know anybody. Of course, things were a little looser back then. Walking into a publisher's office on The Row wasn't like trying to get into Fort Knox," he said matter-of-factly, " but you still needed someone to help you get a foot in the door. A guy named Buddy Carlisle helped me. Now I'm helping you." They had pulled into the motel parking lot, near the office. Rusty held out his hand. As they shook, he offered one final piece of advice: "Take advantage of every possible break you get, meet everybody you can, and stay out there. I know you don't think you're a singer, but you need to be doing open mics every night of the week. It's the only way anyone is gonna know who you are and whether or not you can write. You can write the best dang song anyone on God's green earth ever wrote, but if the only ones who hear it are your mama and your dog, it don't matter how good it is." The dome light came on as JT opened the door to get out. As he looked back at Rusty, he could feel the emotion welling up inside him.

"I don't know how to thank you..." he began in a

thick voice.

Rusty smiled. "Sure you do," he said. "Someday you're gonna meet someone who just pulled in to town and is feeling like they're completely over their head, just like you are now. Help 'em out." JT nodded and slid out of the truck. Rusty powered down the passenger side window.

"Hey," he called. "I almost forgot to give you this." JT saw a business card between two nicotine-stained fingers. "Tomorrow morning, you call this number and talk to Buddy. Tell him Rusty sent you." JT reached into the truck and took the card, and Rusty started to pull away, then stopped. "Hey," he called again. JT walked over to the truck and looked at his new mentor expectantly. "One more thing: CDs, not cassettes. It ain't nineteen eighty."

A brief flash of the brake lights as he rounded the corner of the building, and the truck was out of sight. Now, JT stood outside the motel office, holding the card up to the light, hearing the traffic going by on the interstate at his back. 'Buddy Carlisle, Diamond in the Rough Publishing' it read, with a phone number beneath that. Across the highway, a train horn blatted twice – one long, one short- and was silent. When JT held the card close to his face, he could see that all the dots over the 'i's were tiny diamonds. He walked past the lobby doors toward his room, thinking about that day, and what Rusty's kindness had meant to him, and vowing that he would pay it forward. And about Sarah.

THREE

Now JT stood on this hill, probably his favorite spot in or around Nashville. Many times when he was struggling with a song idea he came to this place, gazing down at the city, trying to clear his head. More often than not, it worked. From his vantage point, he could see LP Field, where the Tennessee Titans play their home games, the AT&T tower –affectionately known as "The Bat Building"- and the sweeping curves of the Cumberland River. He thought back to the day Rusty Sills had approached him in the coffee shop, how desperate he was becoming, how the other man's act of kindness made him feel that everything would work out. But, despite the emotion and gratitude he felt that night, despite his good intentions, he hadn't paid Rusty's kindness forward. True, he had taken his advice about playing open mics and forced himself to get out there and be heard and, eventually, he signed a staff writer deal with a publisher. But he hadn't worked particularly hard at his writing; more often than not, he used his writing chops to meet women. He had learned early on that, in a place like Nashville, having a publishing deal was a tremendously effective aphrodisiac to many of the countless young women who descended on the city each week with dreams of being a hit songwriter dancing in their heads. When he had first signed his deal, he had been very conscientious about writing every day, keeping writing appointments; in short, he had done everything that was expected of him. After a year with his first publisher, a small, one-man operation called Esmond Mills Music, he had been approached by none other than Buddy Carlisle from Diamond in the Rough during a writer's night at the Douglas Corner Café, another popular songwriter hangout. He had called Buddy the day after Rusty had given him the card and Buddy had been very gracious, talking to him at length about his music, his goals, even going so far as to recommend that he speak to Owen Joyce at Esmond Mills, but he had made it clear that JT needed to immerse himself in the business in order to be ready for the big time, to be ready for Diamond in the Rough. While writing for Esmond Mills, JT had scored a couple of album cuts and gained valuable experience in co-writing. Before arriving in Nashville, he had written every note and every word of all of his songs; in Nashville, he learned that, more often than not, songs that get recorded are collaborations. He learned how to write with others, he learned how to compromise, and he learned how to stand his ground when he truly believed in his idea without coming off as stubborn or arrogant. In short, writing at Esmond Mills had been his apprenticeship. Just before his one-year staff writing deal was set to expire, Buddy showed up at an open mic JT was at. He told him that Jim Diamante, the president and founder of Diamond in the Rough, had seen him doing an 'in-the-round' show with three other writers a week or two earlier and been very impressed. Diamante, known professionally as Big Jim Diamond, was a long-time star of the Grand Ol' Opry and had scored a string of self-penned Number One hits in the sixties. Then, tired of life on the road, he had formed a production company in Nashville, working with some of the biggest names in the business, from Waylon Jennings to Johnny Cash and pretty much everyone in between - stars of the highest magnitude. As country music changed, becoming ever-increasingly similar to pop, Big Jim had shifted gears once more, forming his publishing company, Diamond in the Rough Music. Now he was one of the most successful publishers Nashville had ever seen, and his writers had garnered almost too many BMI "Song of the Year" nominations to count and dozens of awards. This was the kind of company JT found himself in. It was a dream-come-true for any writer, and he knew he should thank his lucky stars for the way things had turned out. But, rather than take advantage of all the opportunities he had been blessed with, he had done a one-eighty and was letting it all slip through his fingers.

After a few months of working diligently, he had started to take his situation for granted. He got cocky and began to get a reputation for being unreliable; more than once he missed writing appointments to party with young women he had picked up playing the 'pro writer' card. He never quite promised any of these women he could get them a writing deal, but he didn't discourage their assumptions, either. He started smoking pot, then experimenting occasionally with harder drugs. A writer friend once told him his life was becoming a stereotypical country song: 'All that's missing is your dog dying,' the friend had said. Buddy tried to talk to JT on several occasions, but he had fallen into the party lifestyle and didn't see any reason to change. He had enough success – two top-twenty five songs in the course of six months and a BMI "Song of the Year" nomination – to convince himself that he had "arrived". Like so many people in his situation, JT insisted he didn't have a problem as his life spiraled out of control. It was as if he was inside a tornado funnel and everyone knew it but him. Now, standing high above the city, he realized that, not only did he have a problem, but it was serious, maybe beyond serious. For the briefest of moments he looked down the steep slope of the hill he stood on and wondered if he shouldn't just throw himself over the edge.

Twenty minutes later, he let himself into his apartment north of downtown. As soon as he opened the door, he saw that the "message" light on his answering machine was on, the number four blinking in the darkened room. He walked right past the machine and opened the fridge, looking for a cold drink. He reached for a Coke, then changed his mind and grabbed a beer. He stood there with the door open for a few moments, trying to decide if he should go with the Coke after all, then twisted the cap off the beer and tipped the bottle back. He drank half of it in one swallow, belched, and walked into the living room, passing the answering machine again. He flopped on the couch, aimed the remote at the big screen TV on the wall, and thumbed it on. He sat there, unmoving, for about forty-five minutes, still thinking about his career and the mess he was making of it. He was just about to go get another beer when the phone rang, startling him. He jumped and dropped the empty bottle. It hit the floor and rolled under the couch. JT slumped back and let the call go to his machine. After five rings, he heard his own voice say, "Hey, this is JT. I can't get to the phone, but you know the drill." It was followed by a beep, then Big Jim Diamond's bass voice filled the small room, and he wasn't calling to say 'howdy'.

"Dammit, JT," he thundered, "where in the holy hell are you? You missed another appointment today, with Chuck Kinsella, of all people." Chuck Kinsella had written a string of hits over the past year and Big Jim had been trying to get him and JT together for months. Not only was Kinsella a great writer, but his work ethic was legendary and Jim had hoped some of that would rub off on JT. "Now look, JT, I've left four messages for you already today and I'm losing my patience. It's..." he paused, checking his platinum Rolex, JT assumed, "five-fifteen now. I'll be in my office until about six-thirty. If you get this message, you hightail it over here. We need to talk." He hung up without saying goodbye, the machine beeped again, and the number four changed to five. JT groaned and ran a hand through his hair. Another missed appointment, and this one with one of the hottest, if not *the* hottest, writers in town. He couldn't believe he had done it again. He leaned forward on the couch, head in hands, feeling physically ill. Across the room, the red light on the answering machine glared, accusing, judgemental. Finally, he stood, grabbed his keys off the table near the door, and went out to his truck, determined to make this right.

FOUR

Big Jim Diamond's office looked like a cross between a museum and a trophy showroom. Everywhere you looked, the shelves were covered with statuettes, the walls with plaques and pictures. He was especially proud of the pictures; him with Elvis, who looked impossibly young and trim in his Army fatigues, him with Johnny Cash, him with Buck Owens. They had been contemporaries; it was just as likely that they had sought him out for the pictures as he did them. Soft, tasteful lighting illuminated the pictures and awards that hung on the paneled walls, and the carpeting underfoot was a pale beige, very plush, but understated. The desk was enormous; solid oak front and sides, polished onyx top. More pictures cluttered the desktop; here was Jim with Elvis again -this time while The King was in rehearsals for his 1968 comeback special- Jim with Minnie Pearl, Jim with President Richard M. Nixon. One wall boasted gold and platinum records, some recorded by him, others produced by him, still others written by him. And behind the desk, the man himself: Big Jim Diamond. He had given up the Porter Wagoner look years before, but he still dressed the part of the old-school Country music star; jeans, a brocaded shirt, string tie, ten-gallon hat. On his right pinkie, he wore an enormous gold ring encrusted with diamonds forming the outline of the legendary Ryman Auditorium, Country music's shrine. Big Jim was Country before Country was cool, as the saying goes. More accurately, he was a man who never forgot his roots. He knew what made him 'Big Jim Diamond' and he lived it to the hilt, day-in, day-out. Always in character, he looked like a Teddy bear, a benign grandfather, but underneath that benevolent exterior was a furious temper and an obsessive perfectionism that most people, even those in the business, weren't aware of. Or, if they were aware, they had no clue as to the depth of those characteristics. Simply put, Big Jim was not a man you messed with. Now JT, whom Jim had always treated like a favorite nephew, had done just that. He was firmly on the old man's bad side. Not a good place to be, for sure.

JT got in the truck and then sat, frozen, hand on the key, key in the ignition. How could he possibly make this right? His frenzied mind took out possible solutions, held them up to the light, appraised them, tossed them aside. Jim Diamond was not an idiot, by any stretch of the imagination; there would be no sweet-talking him or, more to the point, no conning him. Finally, still unsure of what he was going to do, but with no real options, JT turned the key, and the truck sputtered and coughed, but didn't start. For a moment, he felt a sense of relief and almost went back inside. But he forced himself to try again and this time the engine turned over and caught. He backed out of his spot, then pointed the truck toward Music Row and the office. At each intersection, he hoped to catch the red light, just for a little more time to think. But, as Luck would have it –as Luck *always* seemed to have it at times like this- he sailed through green light after green light, never even having to slow down. He drove down Charlotte Avenue, cut over on a narrow side street, and then drove a couple of blocks until he reached 16th, in the heart of Music Row. He turned the corner and pulled up in front of Diamond in the Rough Music, which was in an older, but extremely well-kept, office building. Jim had started the company in his house all those years ago, but his success and high profile had necessitated the move to roomier and more professional surroundings early on. He had been the first tenant in this building when it was newly built back in the early seventies. JT sat in his truck, staring at the building, still completely clueless as to what he could do to make amends with his boss. The late afternoon sun beat down on the truck, turning the cabin into a sauna. Finally, with no other alternatives showing themselves, he got out. Just as he threw the door open, a delivery truck blasted by, swerving to avoid it. The driver leaned on the horn and yelled something unintelligible, but never slowed. JT took a deep, shaky breath and got out, this time looking to make sure the way was clear. He walked up the front walkway of the building, between two beautifully manicured plots of Kentucky bluegrass edged with an explosion of flowers. A couple of fat bees droned lazily past him. As he made his way to the door, the lawn sprinklers suddenly popped out of the ground and started spraying with a loud "shoooosh". JT jumped, then realized what the noise was. He glanced around self-consciously, feeling foolish, but there was no one in sight. He reached for the door handle and pulled. Locked. He glanced toward the small parking lot on the side of the building. It was empty, except for a perfectly-restored fifty-nine El Camino. Big Jim's perfectly-restored fifty-nine El Camino, turquoise over white. Head down, JT walked around to the back of the building to the employees' entrance, fishing his key card out of his pocket as he went. He stopped at the door, puzzled. The Gray steel door, always locked after five o'clock, stood open about six inches. JT leaned forward and peered into the darkness.

"Hello?" he called softly. "Jim?" He couldn't explain why, but he felt something was very wrong. He debated going back to his truck and calling the police, but what would he say; 'Hello, I want to report an open door'? He nudged the door, and it swung open further. Just inside to his right there was a short set of carpeted stairs that led to a suite of offices on the ground floor. Actually, they were halfway underground; their windows were at street level. JT couldn't remember who rented space on that floor, although he did recall that one of the girls who worked there was cute. On the left, there was a glass-enclosed directory of the building's tenants on the wall -white push-in letters on a black, plush background- and another short flight of stairs that led up to a landing and the glass door leading into Diamond in the Rough Publishing, which took up the whole first floor. All of the doors had buzzer and card systems because they were always kept locked. Or almost always, apparently. JT stepped all the way into the foyer. After a brief pause, he made his way up the stairs toward Diamond's door. Something was wrong that he couldn't put a finger on. Then it hit him; the light was off in this entry way; he couldn't recall the light ever having been off before, even times he had brought women there in the middle of the night. The system was set up so that, when the last person out set the alarm, the lights came on automatically and stayed on until the alarm was turned off in the morning.

He stopped halfway up the stairs and listened carefully, but heard nothing. He wasn't sure what it was he expected to hear, but the hair on the back of his neck was standing up. If you continued past the office door, another flight of stairs led up to the second floor. JT walked closer to the foot of those stairs and peered around the corner and up into the darkness. He didn't see or hear anything and turned away. He tried the door to Diamond in the Rough, expecting it to be locked, but the lever moved easily, and the door unlatched. The click the latch made seemed very loud to him, standing there in the darkened entryway. He took a deep breath, pulled the door open, and stepped across the threshold.

"Hello?" he called. He glanced down at the phone on the receptionist's desk and noticed one of the indicator lights was lit, meaning someone was on that line. When he leaned over to take a closer look, he saw that the line was labeled 'Jim'. JT's breath escaped in a rush and he walked to the inner office. His relief at everything being okay in the office was tempered by the realization that he was still in a lot of trouble, but that suddenly seemed manageable. At Big Jim's door, which stood open a couple of inches, he paused and knocked. Not receiving a response, he pushed the door open, knowing Jim was talking on the phone.

Except Jim wasn't talking on the phone. Big Jim would never talk on the phone again. JT rushed around the desk, then stopped short. His foot slid on something, but he didn't notice. He couldn't take his eyes from his boss, leaning to one side in his big chair, bleeding from half a dozen wounds. The phone's receiver was dangling halfway between the desk and the floor.

JT watched his own hand reaching slowly for the dropped phone. The whole thing seemed like a dream, or something that was happening to someone else, perhaps on television. JT picked up the phone and put it to his ear.

"Hello?" All he heard was beeping like the phone was off the hook.

JT was still staring at Big Jim Diamond, who was well on his way to that Big Stage in the Sky. Finally, he tore his eyes away and dialed the phone, but the beeping continued unabated. He tried again before he realized he had to clear the line before he could make the call.

FIVE

Staring out the window watching the traffic pass by on West End Avenue, Henry Gray loosened his tie, then sipped his coffee. He winced, moved it away from his lips and blew on it, then tried again. His cell phone was sitting in front of him on the heavily-scarred, Formica-topped table. All of a sudden, it started to vibrate and move slightly. He glanced at it to see who was calling and decided to let it go to voicemail. A waitress walked toward him with a pot of coffee and he immediately placed his hand over his cup.

"No thanks, sweetheart," Henry said, smiling. "I'm waiting for this one to cool down to three hundred degrees so I can drink it. I'll be ready for a refill in about two and a half hours."

The waitress, whose nametag, pinned crookedly to her blue rayon uniform, told the world she was 'Sadie', looked like she had been hired a year or two after the end of the Civil War. She returned his smile warmly and plopped down across the table from him.

"Aw, I'm sorry, Henry, I forgot you had such sensitive lips. Should I put some ice in your hot coffee? You do understand what 'hot' means, right?"

"Nobody likes a wiseass, Sadie," Gray cracked. He pointed at the cup. "It's too hot to handle."

Sadie stood up and gave him a wink. "Just like me, sunshine, just like me." Henry laughed and took another cautious sip while Sadie went to check on her one other customer.

Henry didn't mind that the coffee was too hot to drink because it meant he could sit here and nurse it for a good, long while. Anything to kill time, he thought. Since his wife had moved out a year earlier, he found that he didn't like going home and sitting around the empty house all that much. The place just didn't feel right to him anymore. He had thought more than once about selling, but the market was soft, and he wasn't willing to give it away, so he stayed.

Henry and Priscilla Gray, formerly Priscilla Harvey, had met almost thirty-five years earlier when she moved to Nashville right out of high school in Barbourville, Kentucky, a small town in the heart of coal country. A huge Country music fan, she'd hoped to find a job in the business in hopes of meeting some of her favorite stars and had taken a job waitressing in the meantime. Henry, meanwhile, was working in the same restaurant while waiting to enter the Police

Academy. They'd started dating almost immediately. When Henry got his acceptance letter into the academy, they'd stayed up all night on a hill overlooking downtown Nashville –ironically, the same one JT Wheeler favored- holding one another and planning their future. At first, Priscilla thought being a cop's wife was very exciting, and she reveled in the stories Henry told her when he came home from a patrol shift. She finally found a job working for a publisher as a secretary and their life seemed to be going as planned. However, as time went on, she noticed a change in her husband. He seemed to be more invested in his work and could become very withdrawn around her. When he made detective, things got exponentially worse. While his dogged determination and borderline obsession made him an excellent investigator, Priscilla began to feel more and more like an afterthought to him. Although she had no doubt that Henry had always been faithful to her, it was as if the job had become his mistress. Eventually, she decided things had to change and gave Henry an ultimatum; either her or the job. Henry, who was in the middle of one of the biggest cases of his career, told her they couldn't afford for him to retire yet and asked her to wait a couple more years. Somewhat reluctantly, Priscilla contacted a lawyer, and the marriage ended. She wanted to stay, but at the same time she was realistic enough to know that he would never change. The job was always going to come first, and she had had her fill of playing second fiddle.

Now, all these months later, Henry sat in this downtown coffee shop killing time before he went home. When he finished his coffee, he stood and tossed a ten on the table. He knew Sadie could use the money. Then he walked toward the door.

"So long, Sadie," he called. She was filling salt and pepper shakers at the counter, and now she straightened up.

"Bye, now, Henry," she replied. "You behave yourself."

Henry tipped her a salute. "Will do. You do the same."

"Fat chance," Sadie said, then laughed heartily. *Damned if he don't look just like the Marlboro Man*, she thought, and not for the first time. *If I was twenty years younger...*

The bell over the door jangled as Henry stepped out onto the sidewalk. Just as he did, his phone rang.

"Gray." He listened for a moment, then said, "Okay, got it. On my way."

SIX

Buddy Carlisle was driving toward Diamond in the Rough publishing. As Big Jim's right hand man, he was responsible for the day-to-day running of the office; scheduling writers, studio time, and the like. He did all the time-intensive tasks, thus freeing up Big Jim time to be Big Jim. Shortly after he left that afternoon, he realized he'd left his cell phone on his desk. Luckily, he had stopped to pick up a sandwich at a little market nearby, or he might have been all the way home before he remembered it. He was braking for a stop sign on his way back when he spotted an old pickup truck barreling toward the intersection from his right. Buddy recognized the truck and raised his hand to wave, and then watched, wide-eyed, as JT Wheeler ran straight through the four-way stop without even slowing. Since he was coming from the direction of the office, Buddy assumed Big Jim, finally tired of JT's unreliability, had canned him. Big Jim was a great guy to work for, as long as you worked. Over the years, there had been other guys like JT, guys who seemed to think that signing a staff writing deal was the big prize. But, signing the staff deal was just the first step toward becoming a professional songwriter. Thinking you had 'arrived' just because you became a staff writer was a mistake some people made. The hard work came after you signed on the dotted line. Buddy had heard Big Jim explain it to a new hire years ago who, like JT, thought the deal was the pot of gold at the end of the rainbow.

'Say you signed a contract to play ball with the Yankees," he had said, knowing the writer had grown up near New York City and was a big baseball fan. Jim had a way of tying one thing to another; he felt it made the lessons hit home with greater impact. 'Would you stop taking batting practice because you had a contract, or would you work your ass off to keep it?' That's all it had taken. The writer started working harder than every other writer on staff and wound up collaborating on two Top 10 hits for Garth Brooks within a year. JT, for whatever reason, didn't seem to catch on and now, Buddy assumed, had paid the price with his job. JT was a good writer, but there were a lot of good writers in town. In fact, Big Jim had a saying: 'Good writers are a dime-a-dozen, but great writers are worth their weight in gold.' Buddy smiled at the thought.

As he turned into the parking lot at Diamond in

the Rough, he was shocked to see an ambulance, a fire truck, and three police cars –two marked and one not, all with their lights flashing- along with Big Jim's beloved El Camino. He threw his door open and rushed toward the building, almost stumbling in his haste. A tall man blocked his path before he made it.

"Can I help you?" he asked, flipping open a leather case with a gold badge inside.

"What's wrong? Did something happen to Big Jim?"

"You are?" the man asked him.

"Buddy Carlisle. I work here. Where's Big Jim?"

The cop gave him a sympathetic look and said, "I'm sorry to have to tell you this, sir, but Mr. Diamond is dead."

Buddy put a hand to his forehead; then the other on the fender of one of the police cars to keep himself upright as his knees buckled. The cop reached out a hand to steady him. "Easy," he said.

"Oh, my God," Buddy said. "What happened?"

"It appears Mr. Diamond was shot to death a little while ago. We're waiting for the ME, but it seems pretty straightforward."

"ME?"

"Sorry. Medical Examiner. Sometimes we forget we have our own language. Here she is now." A black commercial van with the word "Coroner" and the Nashville city seal stenciled on the door had pulled in behind the fire truck. An old man with a dead cigar tucked in the corner of his mouth lowered himself to the pavement by hanging on to the side mirror. His progress was exceedingly slow.

"Oh, shit," the cop muttered. Buddy looked at

him, confused. Hadn't the cop said 'she' was here? Now this old timer was approaching them. He shuffled over to where they were standing and nodded.

"Henry."

"Bo," the cop responded. Even though his mind was otherwise occupied, Buddy got the distinct impression the two men didn't care for one another.

"What's the story?" Bo asked, taking the cigar from his mouth and examining it before tucking it back where it had been.

"You're the expert, Bo," the cop replied. "How 'bout you go take a look." Bo's shoulders slumped as he eyed the distance between where he was standing and the entrance to the building. "Second floor, no elevator," the cop called to his departing back.

"I know, God dammit."

Gray looked back at Buddy. "Did you know if Mr. Diamond was expecting anyone this afternoon?" He was loosening his tie and undoing the top button on his shirt. The day was quite warm.

"No. And it's Diamante," Buddy corrected.

"Sir?" The policeman looked at him quizzically.

"His name was James Diamante. Big Jim Diamond was his stage name."

"Oh. Sorry. How do you spell that?" Buddy told him and he jotted it in a small notebook he had taken from the pocket of his shirt.

The cop, who finally introduced himself as Detective Gray, asked a few more questions, then told Buddy he was free to go. Buddy stared at the building, unmoving.

"Can I see him?" he asked, finally.

Gray shook his head. "No, sir, I'm sorry. The

building is a crime scene. No civilians are allowed in." Just then the Medical Examiner came out and motioned Gray to come over. Buddy watched from a distance as they talked. Every few seconds it seemed like one of them –or both- glanced over at him. It was unnerving, and Buddy thought about getting in his car and just getting the hell out of there. Before he could, though, Gray walked back to where he was standing. As he walked toward Buddy, he was fishing in his pocket for something. He finally produced a business card.

"Mr. Carlisle," he said as he offered the card. "This is my information. I'd like you to come into the station tomorrow morning at nine if you don't mind. We have some things to discuss. Is that convenient for you?"

Even though it sounded like a request, Buddy got the feeling his presence at this meeting wasn't optional. He took the card. "Yeah, sure," he agreed, "but why?"

Gray looked at him closely. "Just some routine questions about the business."

"What do you mean?" Buddy gasped, completely shocked. "You think it had to do with the business?"

"Maybe, maybe not. My first instinct would be a botched robbery, but we need to cover all the bases."

Buddy thought about JT blasting through the intersection and suddenly felt faint.

Gray put a hand on his arm to steady him. "Is there someone I can call for you, Mr. Carlisle? Do you need a ride home?" Buddy shook his head, and Gray peered at him closely. "Nine o'clock, then," Gray said. "Are you sure you're alright?" Buddy nodded, so Gray turned and walked back to the building. Buddy dropped the business card into his shirt pocket and went to his car, walking on legs that felt like rubber.

Stopping at the door, Gray watched until Buddy drove out of sight, then went back inside. While they were talking, the crime scene unit had arrived and was processing the scene. The ME had come back in and was leaning against a desk in the outer office. Gray noticed that he seemed like he was having a little trouble breathing and looked sweaty and pale.

"Feeling alright, Bo?" he asked. He certainly wasn't a fan of Bo Shettrick, but he didn't want the old man keeling over, either.

Bo shook his head. "Little asthma, that's all," he answered.

"Do you have an inhaler?" Gray asked.

Bo glared at him. "Why don't you worry about your crime scene, Henry, and mind your damn business?" Henry stared at him, wondering just what his problem was, then shook his head and went back into Big Jim's office. By the time he came out, Bo had left. When the CSU guys finished, the ambulance would deliver the body to the morgue.

SEVEN

Henry Gray had been a member of the Nashville Police Department for almost thirty years, starting out as a patrolman and working his way up through the ranks. He had earned his gold shield eight years earlier. He loved his job, but he had just become eligible for retirement, and he was seriously thinking about it. At fifty-four, he felt like he could start a whole new career that didn't involve shootings and stabbings and other assorted mayhem. He had put in his time and paid the price personally; his marriage had disintegrated as a direct result of his habit of completely immersing himself in every case, becoming consumed by every detail. While that had made him a great detective and given him the highest closure rate in the department, his relationship with his wife had suffered to the point where she had just thrown up her hands in surrender. He had even grown estranged from his two adult children, Mark and Lenore. He hadn't spoken to either of them -or his ex-wife- since the divorce. As the buzzer sounded, and the door unlatched to allow him into the Medical Examiner's office, he wondered if this would be his last case. Not that that would repair his crumbled relationships, but, although he couldn't imagine having been anything other than a detective, he thought maybe it was time to pursue something a little less depressing.

He walked down a short corridor to a door labeled 'Coroner'. He paused for a moment –the smell always got to him- then pushed the door open and walked in. The Medical Examiner who had been at Diamond in the Rough was standing next to a stainless steel table, upon which the sheet-covered body of Big Jim Diamond was resting. Only the dead man's face and shoulders were visible.

"Bo," he said as if the name left a bad taste in his mouth.

"Hello again, Henry," the old man replied. "Always a pleasure." He made no effort to disguise the sarcasm in his voice, which was hoarse from a lifetime of cheap cigars and even cheaper whiskey. It sounded as if he had last slept around the turn of the century and the bags under his eyes did nothing to change that impression. He did seem to have recovered from his asthma attack, however.

"So what are we dealing with here?" Gray asked.

"Well, your victim was shot six times, at close

range, looks to be a twenty-two. Anyone with an IQ over eighty-five could figure the COD." *Then how did you do it?* Gray thought, but he held his tongue.

"Did you recover any slugs?" he asked. Rather than answer him, Bo made a big show of going to the head of the table and getting a pair of tweezers, which he used to pick up something from a metal bowl. He held it up so Henry could see it.

"Here's a slug, slugger," Bo replied, then laughed at his little jape. "Got three more just like it."

"You said six shots. Where are the other two?"

"They went through and through and wound up in the wall," Bo replied. "The CSU boys should be digging them out as we speak."

Henry leaned closer and looked at the slug carefully. "What's that?" he asked.

"What?"

"That fiber?"

Bo looked at the slug. "That's what it is, fiber. They took this one out of his chair. Must be stuffing. Chair guts." He smiled at his little joke.

On the way out to his car, Gray pulled out his cell phone and dialed his partner, Brett Kennedy, who had arrived after him and was still at the scene. They usually rode together but had been running down separate leads in another case this afternoon when Gray took the call about Big Jim. His nose wrinkled at the smell from inside the morgue that seemed to have embedded itself in his clothes, and he made a mental note to drop his suit off at the cleaners on his way home. Then he realized his change of clothes was in a gym bag on his kitchen table and sighed.

"Go," Kennedy answered.

"It's me. You find anything?"

"Not yet. I've got McKenzie and Ziele canvassing the neighborhood to see if anyone saw or heard anything suspicious. So far, nada."

"Okay. Did they get the slugs out of the wall?"

"Yeah, CSU has them."

All right. Let me know if you find anything out. I'm gonna head home. If I don't shower off this morgue stench, I'm gonna puke."

"Will do," Kennedy agreed.

"I've got the guy who was at the scene, Buddy something or other, coming in tomorrow at nine."

"You think he might be the doer?" Kennedy asked; his interest piqued.

"Nah, but I want to see if he can fill in any of the blanks for us. You don't get as big as our victim without pissing a few people off over the years. Maybe he'll let a name slip."

"Maybe. Who did the notification?" Gray asked.

"The Chief said he'd handle it. He knew the vic and his wife."

After a pause, Kennedy asked, "This gonna be your last case?"

"See you tomorrow," Gray responded, then thumbed the phone off. He sat in his car in the morgue parking lot for a minute, then started the engine and drove away. He put down all the windows, convinced he would smell death and formaldehyde for twenty years after he finally walked away from the department.

EIGHT

JT was sitting in his living room with the lights off when someone hammered on his apartment door. He jumped, heart racing, then sat perfectly still, willing whoever it was to go away. The knocking came again, followed by a familiar voice.

"JT! Come on, I know you're home. Answer the door." Buddy. JT stood up and made his way across the room. He couldn't feel his legs, and he was shaking like a leaf. He managed to work the chain off and open the door to find Buddy standing there, white as a sheet. He pushed past JT and strode into the apartment, then turned to him. His hair and eyes were wild.

"What's going on?" he demanded. "You were at

the office. What happened? What did you do?" JT stood silently and stared after Buddy, who had begun to pace back and forth in the small apartment. He stopped suddenly and turned on JT.

"Tell me what happened."

"Buddy," JT began, then stopped, holding out his hands in a pleading gesture. Buddy stared at him expectantly. "I went to the office and he was dead. There was blood everywhere. I called nine-one-one and then got the hell out of there."

"Why would you just take off like that? What if he *wasn't* dead? Did you check for a pulse?"

"No, I just freaked out. I called nine-one-one and…you know…"

"All I know is you flew through that stop sign, then I get to the office and there are cops all over the place, and an ambulance, and Jim's dead." He raked his fingers through his hair and sat down hard on the couch. "Lord." He looked at JT forlornly.

"I swear to God, he was dead when I got there."

"Start at the beginning. And where were you today?"

"I know I missed an appointment…"

"Not just an appointment," Buddy interrupted. "Chuck Kinsella. My Lord, JT." He was gripping the arm of the couch so tightly his fingers had gone white.

"I know, I know. Jim called and left a message on my machine. He was pissed."

"I know he was. Who do you think he yelled at all day?" He jumped up and resumed pacing.

"Anyway, when I got the message, I drove to the office. The El Camino was in the lot, so I went around to the back. The outside door was open. I went in, and all the lights were out. The office door wasn't locked, so I went it. Jim was on the phone."

"You saw him on the phone? So he wasn't dead when you got there."

"No, wait. The light was lit up for his extension. I went into his office and found him."

"I can't believe this is happening," Buddy moaned, rubbing at his face, then remembered the card in his pocket. He pulled it out and handed it to JT. "This detective wants to see me tomorrow morning."

"Why?"

"He wants to ask me some questions."

"What? What does that mean?"

Buddy looked at JT closely and shook his head. "He just said questions about the business."

JT blew out a breath. "Oh, man." He looked at Buddy for a few seconds, then asked, "Did you tell him I was there?"

"No," Buddy replied, then lowered himself onto the arm of the couch. "I can't believe this."

"So they don't know I called it in?" JT asked, on the verge of panic. He had heard stories of people being in the wrong place at the wrong time and getting blamed for all sorts of things. If they knew he had been the nine-one-one caller, they'd have questions for him, too.

"I don't think so. But, you have to talk to him." When JT started to protest, Buddy cut him off. "Look, you were there. You need to tell the cops that. And about the phone call, too. And the doors being open. If he was murdered, the killer must have opened them."

"I can't," JT said, terrified. "How's that going to look? Jim called me into the office, probably to fire me, and now he's dead. I've never heard him so mad."

Buddy rubbed his forehead. "Oh, God," he said, "I wonder if Margie knows."

"Margie? What about Bev?" JT asked.

Buddy shot him a look, then said, "He was going to divorce Bev. She's a..." He didn't finish the thought.

"So what happens to the company?" JT ventured. Despite everything that was going on, he was still thinking how he was going to cover his butt. *If Jim's gone, I should still have my gig,* he thought. He knew it was wrong to be looking at things from that angle, but he couldn't help it.

"Are you flipping kidding me?" Buddy exploded, flying up and causing JT to recoil. That was as close as he had ever heard the church-going Buddy come to swearing. "Jim is dead and all you can think about is yourself. You're pathetic." He strode to the door but, before he opened it to leave, he turned around. "You know, JT, when you got here, you were a decent guy. What happened to you?" Buddy pulled the door open and went out, slamming it behind him and leaving JT to ponder that question.

He leaned against the door, wondering what his immediate future held for him, then went to the fridge and grabbed a beer.

NINE

At five minutes before nine, Buddy walked into Nashville Police Central District Headquarters on Broadway, right next to the Bridgestone Arena, home of the city's professional hockey team. He was very nervous, although he wasn't sure why that should be. He walked up to the information desk and asked for Detective Gray. The officer manning the desk gestured toward a row of hard plastic chairs lining one wall.

"Have a seat," he said. "I'll let him know you're here."

Buddy had sat down before he realized the officer hadn't asked for his name. He debated whether or not he should go back to the window when a door on the wall opposite where he was seated -to the right of the window- opened. Another uniformed officer peered out at him.

"Mr. Carlisle?" Buddy nodded. "Come with me, please."

Buddy followed him to a security checkpoint. The officer turned to him.

"Empty your pockets, please." He handed Buddy a plastic bin and waited while he put his wallet, keys, and phone into it. "Watch and belt, too," he said. Buddy complied, then looked at his left hand. "You can keep your ring on," the officer said, sounding a bit bored. It was obvious he had done this more times than he could count. He placed the plastic bin on a conveyer belt that carried it through a large scanner. "Step through, please."

Buddy stepped through an electronic archway toward another officer who was waiting on the other side with a detection wand, but the alarm didn't sound. The first officer picked up the plastic bin when it came through and handed it to Buddy, who retrieved his belongings and slipped them back into various pockets, put on his belt and watch, and then looked at the officer expectantly.

"Follow me, sir," he said, and Buddy fell in behind him as they made their way down a long hallway lined with offices. When they reached one with a sign next to the door that read 'Detective Division', the officer motioned to Buddy to go in. Gray was sitting at a cluttered desk with his back to the door. The officer accompanying Buddy rapped on the doorframe, and Gray turned in his seat, then stood when he saw him.

"Mr. Carlisle," he said warmly, extending his hand. "Thank you for coming in," he added, as if there had been any choice. He picked up a stack of file folders from a chair placed next to the desk, then turned to a second, younger officer. "This is Detective Kennedy. Brett, Mr. Carlisle." Kennedy and Buddy shook.

"Please, have a seat," Gray said. As soon as Buddy sat down, he asked, "Coffee?"

Buddy, whose stomach was doing flips, shook his head. "No, thank you," he said.

Gray settled back behind the desk. "I'll try to make this as quick as possible," he said, pulling a yellow legal pad from a stack of pads, notebooks, you name it. He took a pen from his shirt pocket. "Okay, the first thing, and I'm very sorry to have to tell you this, is that Mr. Diamante was shot several times. That doesn't jibe with our initial feeling that this was a robbery-gone-wrong, but rather a premeditated killing." He watched Buddy's reaction carefully.

"Why would someone do that?" he asked in an almost inaudible voice, shocked.

"We're not sure yet," Gray said, still watching. "We were hoping you might have an idea."

Suddenly the force of what he was saying hit Buddy, and he slumped in his chair, his hand covering his mouth.

"Why would anyone kill him? I can't believe that." He looked to be on the verge of tears.

"I understand, and I'm sorry, but that's what happened. Can you think of anyone who would have any reason to hurt him?"

Buddy shook his head vehemently. "No, no one.

Jim was loved and respected in the business. I can't believe this."

"Well, we haven't ruled out the possibility of a robbery, but we don't think that was it. Did he keep large sums of cash on the premises?"

Buddy looked confused for a moment, then shook his head. "No, of course not. Music publishing isn't a cash business." All the while Gray was making notes on the pad.

"Did he have any disputes with anyone?"

Buddy shook his head again. "No, no one."

Now, for the first time, Gray sensed he was holding back. He looked him over appraisingly. "None at all?"

"Well, people don't always agree with one another, but nothing that would make someone kill him."

"Did you and Mr. Diamante argue about anything?"

"What?" Buddy had reached up to wipe away a tear, but he stopped, his hand hovering halfway to his face. "NO! How can you think that?"

"Calm down, sir," Gray said, now very stern and businesslike, his initial friendly demeanor quickly evaporating. "These are routine questions."

"Do I need a lawyer?" Buddy whispered, incredulous.

Gray didn't answer for several long seconds, just held Buddy's gaze. It was intended to be disconcerting and was. Buddy shifted uncomfortably in his chair. "No," he said finally, then added, "Not at the moment." He let the words sink in for the desired effect. "Now," he said, "have there been any incidents, you know, things that would make him angry or upset in any way, things that might precipitate an argument? And before you answer that, let me tell you that I've done a little digging, and I know all about your boss's temper. It's actually legendary."

Buddy stared at him, then shook his head, but he was thinking about the situation with JT. Jim had ranted and raved all day about the missed appointment. Getting one of his writers a writing session with Chuck Kinsella had been something of a coup, even for a man with Jim's connections. He had to call in a couple of favors to make it happen and then JT had been a no-show. The more he thought about it, the more Buddy realized that he had never seen Big Jim so angry. And after working with him for the better part of thirty years, he had seen the big man's temper on many occasions. Then he remembered JT running through the stop sign, clearly in a hurry to get away from the office.

Gray watched him with interest, almost able to see the interior struggle play out on his face. He rubbed his chin and waited.

"Well, I mean, he was kind of upset yesterday," Buddy finally allowed.

Bingo! Gray thought. "And what, exactly, happened to make him upset?" he asked casually.

"Just something with one of the writers," Buddy said, trying not to divulge too many details. He didn't think JT had anything to do with Jim's murder, and he was loathe to be the one who gave his name to the cops. He figured JT was right; it wouldn't look good.

Gray waited for him to elaborate. One of the first lessons he had learned as a cop was to give witnesses and suspects time to speak. He and his first partner when he came on the job, an old school cop named Lonnie Bergen, had picked up a robbery suspect one time. Bergen, who had a reputation on the street for being fair with suspects, let Henry handle the interview. Henry quickly got frustrated with what he perceived to be the man's lack of cooperation and threatened to rearrange various body parts. The suspect, in turn, asked for a lawyer and the cops' job became that much more difficult. Bergen backed his new partner's play, but when they were alone, he promised to have Henry reassigned to a horse stable "without a shovel". He was absolutely furious. Once he cooled off, he explained the nuances of interrogation, including giving the person you were interviewing time to formulate his or her thoughts. It was a lesson Henry only needed it explained to him that one time. Now, as usual, his patience paid off.

"One of our writers missed an appointment. Jim was kind of ticked off."

Gray didn't show any reaction at all, just watched Buddy. "An appointment?" he asked.

"Yeah, writers write by appointment."

"That's interesting. I would have thought they just sat in a room and waited for inspiration to strike."

"Everybody thinks that," Buddy said. "When you get to this level, writers get together by appointment." When Gray didn't respond, he said, "Everybody's really busy. It's not like you can just call somebody up and say, 'Let's write'. Everyone you called would probably already be writing with someone else."

"So who was this writer that didn't show for his appointment?"

Buddy paused. Gray waited him out; certain the information would be forthcoming. "JT, uh, Justin." Buddy said finally in a quiet voice, then hastily added, "But, he couldn't have had anything to do with it." He hadn't wanted to involve JT, but he felt like he had no choice. He was hoping JT would contact the cops on his own, but that hadn't happened. Gray watched him, still convinced there was more to the story because Buddy, although he was trying to appear cool, calm, and collected was getting more fidgety by the minute. Gray bided his time, then, when he thought Buddy was ready, leaned back in his chair, hands folded across his middle.

"Justin who?" Gray asked.

"Wheeler. JT Wheeler," Buddy said in an even softer voice.

"Why don't you tell me about what happened with Mr. Wheeler." Buddy slumped in the chair. He hadn't wanted to get into this, but now he felt like he had no choice.

"JT had an appointment yesterday, but he didn't show up. Jim was pretty pissed off."

"A writing appointment?"

"Yeah."

"Why didn't he show up?" Gray asked.

"I don't know. Jim kept calling him, but his cell was turned off, so he started calling his apartment."

"How many times did he call?"

"I don't know, a few."

"Well, how many? Four, five, ten?" He watched Buddy and waited.

"I don't know. I guess maybe five or ten to the cell and a few more to the apartment."

"Okay, so Mr. Diamante called this Wheeler guy, what, fifteen times?"

"I don't know. Maybe." Buddy shook his head. "I guess so, yeah."

"So he was more than 'pretty pissed off', wouldn't you say?" Buddy nodded miserably. Gray rubbed his chin again, thoughtful. He looked at the notes he had written on the pad, then back at Buddy. "Did he leave Mr. Wheeler any messages?" Buddy looked extremely uncomfortable. He felt like Gray was now leading him toward a predetermined point. "Mr. Carlisle? Any messages?"

"Yeah, he wanted him to go to the office."

"I see. And did Mr. Wheeler show up?"

"I don't know."

"You don't? Are you sure, Mr. Carlisle?

"God," Buddy sighed, and put his hands over his face, then dropped them and blurted, "I saw JT near the office, but there's no way he could have done this."

Gray stayed calm. "What time did you see him, Mr. Carlisle?"

"Just before I got there," Buddy allowed, his voice almost too quiet to hear.

Gray didn't say anything for at least a minute. Finally, he asked, "Do you have an address for Mr. Wheeler?" He didn't wait for an answer, just slid the pad across the desk and offered Buddy a pen. "Jot it down for me, would you?" he said, now back to his friendly tone.

As soon as Buddy had finished, Gray ended the interview abruptly. "Okay," he said, standing and offering his hand. "I think that's all we need for now. Thank you for your cooperation." He plucked another card from a holder on his desk and held it out to Buddy. "If you think of anything else, give me a call."

Buddy accepted the card wordlessly. The same officer who had led him to the office materialized next to him. "Officer Carr will show you out," Gray said. Buddy stared at him briefly, then got up from the chair like an old man, holding the arm to steady himself.

Gray turned to Kennedy, who was already shrugging into his suit jacket and had his keys out.

"Let's go."

TEN

"Okay. What's that address?" Kennedy asked.

Gray glanced down at the legal pad where Buddy had written it. "Eight-fifty-five Elmhurst, apartment twelve." Kennedy aimed the car for the highway. When Route 40 turned to the west, he got on 65. Two minutes later, he exited and began to navigate the surface streets.

Eight-fifty-five was a sturdy-but-well-worn, two-story brick building, the brick interspersed with sections of dingy white vinyl siding. It sat smack in the middle of about a half acre of asphalt with a few tired-looking patches of grass thrown in for good measure. What few trees and shrubs dotted the property looked like lost causes and most of the cars in the lot appeared to be over ten years old. Kennedy drove in, and they quickly spotted number twelve, which was right at the bottom of a metal staircase in desperate need of a coat of paint. He pulled into an empty spot next to an old pick-up with a fading Community College of Rhode Island sticker plastered across the back window. Gray knocked on the door to JT's apartment. There was no response, so he knocked again. This time, he heard a muffled voice through the door, although he couldn't understand what the person inside had said. Just as he was ready to knock again, the door swung open. The man who had opened the door blinked against the bright sunshine, then raised his arm to shield his eyes. He was wearing boxers and nothing else and appeared to have been drinking, as evidenced by his flushed complexion.

"Can I help you?" the man asked. Gray flipped open his badge holder.

"Justin Wheeler?" JT, who had paled instantly at the sight of the badge, tried to answer, but nothing came out when he opened his mouth. Finally, he just nodded.

"I'm Detective Gray and this is Detective Kennedy. We'd like to ask you a few questions about James Diamante." JT stood there silently, his eyes darting back and forth between the two cops.

"Get dressed, Mr. Wheeler," Gray said. "You need to come down to the station."

"Am I under arrest?" JT asked.

"We need you to come downtown," Gray said, avoiding the question. This was another technique he learned from Lonnie Bergen; keep the suspect off-balance.

JT turned away from the door. As he did, he reached out and put his hand on it as if was going to close it. Kennedy stepped forward and grabbed the knob.

"Why don't we just leave that open," he said.

JT looked like he might vomit. "Sorry," he said, then walked deeper into the apartment and found some clothes balled up on the couch. He slipped on a pair of faded jeans and a Titans t-shirt, then picked up a scuffed pair of work boots. He sat down and pulled them on, then stood up. Kennedy stayed just inside the door to make sure JT didn't do anything stupid, like try to go out the back door if there was one.

"Let's go," Gray said as JT walked back to where they were standing. Gray walked to the car, followed by JT and then Kennedy. He opened the back door, and JT slid inside, his face still ashen. Neither officer talked on the way to the station; not to JT, not to each other. When they pulled into a spot behind the precinct, Kennedy got out and opened JT's door.

"Let's go," he said. He marched JT into the building with Gray trailing behind them. Kennedy had a hand on JT's arm, not because he expected him to try anything, but to make sure he knew he wasn't just there for a friendly chat, but that this was a serious situation for him.

Inside, they walked him to the darkest, dreariest interrogation room in the building. JT sat stiffly in a metal chair, looking back and forth between the two detectives, who stood a few feet apart from one another. Kennedy was near the door; arms folded as if he expected JT to make a break for it. Gray sat on the edge of the table that JT was seated at, next to him. JT licked his lips. *Why aren't they saying anything?* he wondered. If they were remaining silent to make him nervous, it was working and then some. JT began tapping his left foot. Still, neither detective spoke. He ran a hand through his hair and wasn't at all surprised when it came away damp. He was distantly aware of sweat running down his sides beneath his shirt. Finally, he couldn't take it anymore.

"Do I need a lawyer?" he asked. The detectives exchanged a glance.

"Do you need a lawyer?" Gray repeated, seemingly puzzled. "I don't know. Do you?"

JT swallowed hard. "I didn't do anything," he said in a small voice.

Gray leaned forward. "What was that?" he asked.

JT shook his head, then tried again. "I didn't do anything."

"I see," Gray said, reasonable, friendly. "Well, rather than waste each other's time, why don't I tell you what we already know and maybe you can help fill in the blanks." JT just stared at the table. "Okay?" Gray asked. JT nodded almost imperceptibly. "Okay, so we know that you blew off a very important appointment yesterday and your boss was royally pissed. So far, so good?" JT glanced up at him, then looked away. Gray noticed his eyes looked glassy, almost as if he were in shock. Or high, he thought.

"We also know he called you multiple times to ream your ass." No response. "Further, we know he wanted you in his office, probably to fire you. Stop me if any of this doesn't ring a bell with you." JT continued to stare down. "We know someone shot him six times while he was sitting in his office." He paused for dramatic effect. "And we have a witness who places you near the scene after he was killed." Channeling his old partner, Lonnie, Gray waited JT out.

A solid two minutes of silence later, JT broke. "I went to talk to him, but the door was unlocked when I got there."

Gray nodded at him to continue. "Why don't you start at the beginning?"

JT took a deep breath and blew it out. "I missed the appointment because I was...I was," he shrugged, "out." Kennedy had begun taking notes.

"Out where?" Gray asked. JT slumped, defeated.

"I was with someone, a woman. We were in bed all afternoon."

"Her name?" Gray asked. When JT didn't answer, he leaned toward him. "Look, we have to check your story," he said, sounding almost like a friend, a confidante. "Give us a name." JT shook his head. "You're not doing yourself any favors here, pal," Gray said, his voice suddenly tinged with impatience. "Her name. Now."

"She's married," JT said.

Gray shook his head and looked at Kennedy, who shook his in return, then got right up in JT's face. "I don't care if she's married, single, from another planet, or has six heads and three arms. Either give us a name or your next stop is lockup."

JT's eyes grew wide. "I didn't murder Jim," he wailed.

"Fine, so you said. But until you tell us who you were with, you don't have an alibi, either."

JT stared at him, not knowing what to do. "God,"

he said finally, hanging his head. "Mindy Barrish." Kennedy wrote it down.

"Two r's?"

"Yes."

"Phone number?"

"Please," JT pleaded.

"Just give us the number," Gray said, no longer making any effort to hide his aggravation. JT told him, and Kennedy wrote that down as well. JT was slumped so far down in his chair he looked like he was in danger of sliding under the table.

"God," he breathed and put his hand over his eyes, then pushed it through his hair, leaving it standing up in places. He told the rest of his story, leaving out the part about Doug Barrish coming home while he was still in bed with Mindy and him running out the back door like a coward and a thief, carrying his clothing.

When he was done, Gray nodded. "That's it for now," he said. "But, don't leave town in case we need to talk to you again." JT looked at him but didn't say anything. In truth, he didn't know what to say. "I'll have an officer drive you home," Gray added.

"Okay," JT mumbled and stood up. He wasn't surprised that the back of his shirt and the seat of his jeans were sticking to him. He was sweating bullets.

As soon as the door closed behind him, Gray asked, "How much more do you think he knows?"

"Quite a bit more than he's telling us," Kennedy replied.

"Let's give him a couple of days and have another go at him."

"He may know more, but I don't think he's the doer," the junior detective said.

Gray immediately nodded. "You're right about that. He doesn't have the balls."

ELEVEN

Rusty Sills was half in the bag, maybe more. He had started drinking –heavily- as soon as he had gotten the news that Big Jim Diamond was dead. Jim and Buddy Carlisle had helped Rusty get his career off the ground not long after he had arrived in Nashville with twenty dollars in his pocket, a battered Martin acoustic guitar slung over his back, and a notebook full of song lyrics. He had managed to get home at closing time, but had parked himself back on a barstool at ten this morning. Now, three hours later, he sat, bleary-eyed in a downtown watering hole. The bartender was keeping a close eye on him.

"Rusty, I think you're done, buddy."

"Screw that, compadre," Rusty growled. "I'll tell you when I'm done. To Big Jim," he toasted. He raised his glass, sloshing most of his drink on the bar, and threw back what was left. "Again!" he cried, but the bartender shook his head as Rusty licked Bourbon off the back of his hand.

"Rusty, I can't. How about some coffee and a sandwich? When's the last time you ate something?" He looked up as the front door opened. A woman came in, briefly silhouetted by the midday sun. The light outlining her slender body made her look ethereal and angelic. She walked over to where Rusty was sitting, climbed up on the stool next to him, and put a hand on his arm. She nodded at the bartender.

"Sonny."

"Dixie Lee," he responded.

"Thanks for calling," she said.

"No problem. I figured you'd want to know."

Dixie Lee Wrenn -the extra 'n' was for naughty, she liked to say- also known as The Carolina Songbird - leaned close to Rusty. "You've had enough, Rusty. You getting all pie-eyed ain't gonna bring him back."

Rusty started to cry quietly. "He's gone, Dix, he's gone."

"I know, I know," she murmured in a soothing tone as she patted his hand. She noticed his nails had a ragged, *bitten* look.

"I can't believe he's gone." He thrust his glass toward the bartender. "Hit me, Sonny."

Sonny shook his head. "No, sir. Time to go, Rusty."

Rusty turned to look at Dixie Lee. "He's gone, Dix," he sobbed. "He's really gone."

"Good riddance to bad rubbish," she muttered, shocking him to silence. She jumped down off her stool as he glared at her, wounded.

"How can you say that?" he finally whispered raggedly.

"Rusty, you can romanticize the old bastard six ways to Sunday, but the bottom line is he was a philandering, mean-spirited, song-stealing, son of a bitch. Ain't no two ways about it." She put her hands on her hips as if that somehow served to emphasize her point.

Rusty pressed his lips together, then moaned, "He was my friend, Dixie Lee. He gave me my start in this town." When she didn't respond, he added, "He helped you, too. Or have you forgotten?"

"He helped himself to me, Rusty. That's what he did."

Suddenly Rusty lashed out with his right hand, but he was drunk and slow, and Dixie dodged the slap easily. Sonny grabbed Rusty's arm and pinned it against the bar.

"That's it, Dixie Lee," he said. "You got two choices, hon. You can take him home, or I can call the cops. I don't need this." He shook his head again. "It's bad enough he showed up here at ten in the goddamn morning. And this after he closed me down last night."

Dixie Lee laughed and shook her head. "Well, maybe you should have thought of that before you poured him all them drinks, Sonny." She grabbed Rusty by the arm and hauled him up off his barstool. "All right, sad sack," she said with as much false cheer as she could muster. "Let's get you out of here while you can still walk. I hope."

Dixie Lee put her arm around Rusty's waist, then grabbed his arm and laid it on her shoulders. She half carried, half dragged him to the door of the bar, then out into the sunshine.

"Damn!" Rusty cried and threw an arm up to shield his eyes. The sudden movement almost made them fall, but Dixie Lee righted the ship before it capsized. They made their way down the sidewalk until they reached her car, and she managed to pour him into the passenger seat and get the seatbelt on him. They made quite a pair; the tall, gangly -and very drunk- man and the diminutive woman with the mop of blonde hair and fading good looks. She went around to the other side and climbed in.

"I'm sorry, Dixie Lee," Rusty mumbled, his chin on his chest.

"It'll be okay, Rusty," she said compassionately, patting him on the knee, then added, "Just don't you go puking in my car, you hear me?" She put the car in gear and pulled away from the curb. Before she had gone a full block, Rusty was snoring away noisily. Dixie glanced at him and shook her head.

TWELVE

Two hours after questioning JT, Gray and Kennedy stood on the doorstep of Big Jim's twelve million dollar home in Belle Meade, a tony suburb southwest of Nashville. Gray pushed the doorbell, and they waited in the mid-day heat. Both men were looking around a little wide-eyed at the vast, well-maintained grounds. To the right of the house, there was a corral with two painted horses in it. Beyond that was a barn much bigger than either of their houses. *Probably nicer inside, too*, Gray mused.

"So this is how the other half lives, huh?" Kennedy said with a whistle.

"I guess," Gray said. "It would probably take six

cops to afford this place. And two of them would have to be crooked."

"I knew I was in the wrong business," Kennedy lamented. "I should have been a music publisher. Or a drug dealer."

"There's still time," Gray joked. "You're a young man."

Kennedy was about to reply when the front door opened, revealing an extremely attractive young woman. "Yes?" she asked. She looked to be in her late twenties, with long, honey blond hair cascading over her tanned shoulders and a stunning figure. She was wearing a halter top and tiny shorts that showed off her assets beautifully.

"Miss Diamante? I'm Detective Gray, and this is Detective Kennedy. We're here about your father."

"Oh my God, did something happen to my daddy, too?" the woman said, then laughed at their confused expressions. She left no doubt she was playing with them. "Oh, you mean Big Jim? He was my husband, gentlemen, not my father." She stepped to the side so they could enter the house, which was even more impressive inside than out. They were standing in a marble-tiled foyer under an enormous glass chandellier. The residence stretched out on both sides of them, tastefully decorated with what appeared to Henry's eye to be nothing but antiques. A staircase directly in front of them would have made the set designer from 'Gone with the Wind' insane with jealousy.

Mrs. Diamante seemed to enjoy watching their reaction to her home, but finally she said, "You'll have to forgive me, gentlemen, but I only have a few minutes. All these arrangements, you know."

Gray nodded. "Yes, ma'am, we understand. We appreciate you're taking the time to see us. We're very sorry for your loss." He was still a little dazed. He had been expecting the woman he had seen in pictures on Diamante's desk, a middle-aged, almost matronly woman on the north side of sixty. Certainly not the half-dressed goddess standing before him now.

"Hmmm? Oh, yes, thank you. Now, what did you want to talk to me about?"

"Well, as Chief Wall told you, your husband was murdered."

"Yes, Martin made me aware of that." She paused to make sure they noticed her casual use of the chief's given name. Message: 'I am not someone to be trifled with.'

"Well, we're trying to determine if there was anyone in particular that you know of who might have had any sort of problem with your husband. Maybe a business deal gone wrong, something of that nature?"

The widow chuckled. "The only business Jim had a problem with was the business between his legs." She put a hand on Gray's arm, pleased at the shocked look he tried to conceal and winked. "Sometimes it wound up in places it didn't belong."

Gray and Kennedy exchanged a glance. Beverly Diamante was certainly not your typical widow. She seemed to understand the look.

"Let me explain something, gentlemen. Jim and I were married for the sake of his position in the music business. When he met me, he dumped that frumpy old bag he was married to, mainly because I looked so much better on his arm at awards shows." She placed her hands under her ample breasts and pushed up slightly. "He gave me these for our first anniversary," she said proudly. After a pause to allow that to sink in, she added, "Jim was a man who would accept nothing less than perfection." She glanced down at herself, then looked at Gray and winked. "As you can see," she added.

"Yes, um, well," Gray stammered awkwardly, completely at a loss for words.

Beverly smiled graciously. "Now, if there's nothing else..." Gray and Kennedy stepped out back out into the heat.

"Uh, no, ma'am. I guess not. Thank you for...." By the time he said, "your time," she had closed the door firmly in their faces.

"Wow," Kennedy said.

"Yeah," Gray agreed. "Wow. What the hell was that?"

"You got me," Kennedy replied with a shake of the head. They stood staring at the door for a few moments, then walked back to where their car was parked. "Now what?" Kennedy asked, sliding behind the wheel.

"I think I'd like to go take another look around the office."

Kennedy put the car in gear and drove through the circular driveway. After a brief silence, he glanced over at Gray, who was staring out the window. "I think the grieving widow took a shine to you."

Gray grunted. "What a psycho, huh? I think 'the grieving widow', as you put it, just jumped way up on my list of suspects. Either she or whoever she's been sleeping with."

"Why do I get the feeling that's going to be a long,

long list?" Kennedy sighed, shaking his head.

"Did you notice how she let us in just far enough to get a pretty good look around, and then maneuvered us back toward the door?"

"Yeah, I guess the widow Diamante likes to be in control and wants to make sure you know it, too."

"So maybe she didn't like the fact that her husband was getting a little something on the side."

"She probably couldn't fathom him wanting anyone else if he could be with her. I'm guessing there isn't room in her little world for that possibility. 'Jim was a man who would accept nothing less than perfection,'" he mimicked. "Jesus." They drove in the direction of Music Row for a couple minutes. Then Kennedy asked, "You think we should bring her in for a chat? Maybe she won't be quite so sure of herself when she's in our house instead of hers."

Gray shook his head. "No, you heard the way she dropped the chief's name. That was a message that they're friends, and we'd better not screw with her. If we decide to bring her in, we're going to have to run it by him first."

"I hate this political garbage," Kennedy spat. "Police work should be police work. It shouldn't matter who your friends are."

"Amen to that, brother," Gray responded, then shrugged. "But it is what it is. Let's go grab some lunch. I'm starving."

THIRTEEN

Gray and Kennedy were sitting in the car, pulled into a spot at a Sonic drive-in. They had already ordered and were waiting for their food to come out.

"What strikes you odd about the office?" Kennedy asked.

Gray pursed his lips and appeared to be deep in thought. "A few things," he said. He held up his hand and extended his thumb as if hitchhiking. "One, he had a million pictures between the desk and the walls, so why aren't there any of Beverly? Lord knows she's photogenic. He had two of his first wife, but none of the young, beautiful one." Index finger. "Two, he was sitting at his desk on the phone when he was killed.

There's no sign he even tried to get up, so why did the perp feel the need to empty the gun?" Middle finger.

"Three, how did the killer get into what was supposedly a locked building? Did they have a key?" Ring finger. "Four, why would anyone hate this guy so much that they felt it necessary to shoot him six times? What could he have done that he deserved that? Six shots makes it personal."

Kennedy waited. "No pinky?" he asked with a smile.

Gray shook his head. "Not yet, but give me time." Gray's phone rang. Kennedy could only hear his side of the conversation, but it was clear what was going on. "Yes, sir. Yes, sir. I understand. Right away." He ended the call. "Shit! So much for lunch." Just then, a waitress emerged from the building with a tray and headed for their car. When she got close enough, Gray dropped a twenty and a ten on the next to the food. "Sorry, Chandra," he said. "Duty calls. Keep the change." He drove off, leaving the waitress standing in the parking lot with the tray full of food and a confused look on her face.

"That must have been the chief," Kennedy observed, "'cause you just skipped out on a double bacon burger."

"None other," Gray replied. He wants to see us. Five minutes ago." Since time was suddenly of the essence, Gray turned on the blue lights in the car's grille. Within minutes, they were pulling up to the curb at the side of the police station. Gray swiped his keycard, and they entered the building through an unmarked metal door. Inside, they quickly went up two flights of stairs and down the hall to the chief's office.

The door to the anteroom was open and Gladys Hilliard, the chief's secretary for more than thirty years -predating the current chief by at least twenty- looked up when they walked in.

"He's waiting for you," she said, pasting what passed for a smile on her thin, heavily-seamed face.

"I hate being summoned to the principal's office," Gray muttered under his breath, then rapped on the second door, which had Martin Wall, Chief of Detectives stenciled on the pebbled glass.

"Come," a gruff voice answered from inside the office. The detectives entered the department's version of the sanctum sanctorum; someplace very few rank and file officers ever saw, and even fewer aspired to see. Usually, a visit to the chief's office meant you were about to be handed discipline, although Gray and Kennedy weren't worried about that. There were three other high-ranking officers in the room beside the chief; two majors and a captain.

Wall lifted his chin at Kennedy. "Close that door, Detective." Kennedy closed the door quietly and turned back. He was aware his hands were sweating. "I'm sure you two are already aware that I've taken a personal interest in the Big Jim Diamond case," Wall said. Gray nodded. "This is a very high profile situation, gentlemen, and all eyes are upon us."

"Yes, sir, we're aware of that," Gray said. As the senior officer, he always spoke for them.

"I want this thing investigated to within an inch of its life and then I want you to investigate it some more. Don't cut any corners, don't take any shortcuts."

"Are you insinuating we normally do? Sir?" Gray said in a soft, neutral voice. Though his tone was mild, the challenge he was issuing was clear. He was offended at being dragged in like this. Kennedy stifled a grimace. The chief fixed his gaze on Gray.

Unexpectedly, he smiled. "I guess when you're as close to retirement as you are, you feel free to speak your mind, eh, Detective?"

"I just want to make sure there are no misunderstandings about our expertise and professionalism."

"Get off your high horse, Detective," the chief retorted, his smile fading as quickly as it had appeared. "If I weren't convinced you boys were the best ones for this case, you wouldn't be on it. You didn't catch it by accident, you know."

"Thank you, sir," Gray nodded. "We appreciate your confidence in us."

"I just want to make sure you understand how high profile this thing is, that's all." Gray nodded again. "Big Jim Diamond was huge in this town, the biggest of the big." The chief went on to talk about the case, inquire as to any progress they'd made, then revealed the true reason behind this conversation, although it wasn't exactly what Gray and Kennedy had expected.

"I'm aware that you've spoken to Beverly Diamante," he said. "I want her handled with kid gloves, is that clear?" This time both detectives nodded. *Yeah*, Gray thought, *that's clear*. In other words, hands off the beautiful widow, but Wall surprised him. "That being said, I think you should be taking a very close look at Miss Beverly. Maybe she had nothing to do with it. In fact, I hope she had nothing to do with it, but don't rule anything out. My gut tells me she should be right at the top of your suspect list."

"She is," Gray assured him, but something in his tone brought a slight smile to the chief's face.

"You're surprised that I suspect her," Wall said. Gray shrugged, and the chief said, "People like to forget I was a damn good detective in my day. My instincts are still solid." Wall had been a highly-decorated lieutenant in Memphis before he began his climb up the "brass ladder", eventually being named to the top spot of the detective division in Nashville ten years earlier.

"I'm not some bureaucrat, gentleman," he went on. "I made my bones in Memphis." Gray thought it odd he would use that phrase, 'made my bones', since it is more commonly used in mob or gang parlance, referencing someone's first murder. Always the detective, he filed it away even though he was sure there was nothing to it. "Mrs. Wall and I were friends with Jim and Marjorie. For our money, Beverly was just a gold-digging tramp. And there were rumors Jim had finally come to his senses about her. If they divorced, the pre-nup left her with a small allowance. If he died, though..." He didn't need to complete his thought.

"Got it," Gray remarked. "Anything else, Chief?"

Wall shook his head. "Get back to work."

On their way back down the stairs, Kennedy asked, "What do you think?"

Gray shrugged. "I'm not sure. First he says handle her gently. Then he says she should be at the top of the suspect pool. He can claim he's not a bureaucrat, but he's certainly a politician. I don't know, maybe he figures he better cover his ass no matter which way it turns out."

"I guess," Kennedy said as he pushed the door to the sidewalk open. "You scared the crap out of me, talking to him like that."

Gray smiled. "What's he going to do, fire me?"

FOURTEEN

The detectives were sitting at their respective desks when another officer called to them.

"Guys, pick up line two. Possible lead on your case." Gray reached for his phone and punched the flashing button.

"Detective Gray. How can I help you?" He cradled the phone between his ear and shoulder and motioned to Kennedy to toss him a pen. He caught it deftly and began to make notes on his desk blotter. "Uh huh. Yep. Uh huh. Okay, we'll stop by. Okay, thanks." He hung up and looked at Kennedy, who was watching him closely. "A guy who claims he was on the phone with Big Jim when the shooting went down.

He thinks he might have heard Jim arguing with the shooter." He stood and took his jacket off the back of his chair. "Let's roll."

In the car, Kennedy glanced over at his partner. "So where to?"

"Hendersonville."

"To see?" Kennedy asked, arching one eyebrow.

"Mr. Copeland, aka 'Cowboy Carl'," Gray replied, grinning.

Kennedy shook his head. "Of course," he deadpanned. "Yee-freakin'-haw!"

Cowboy Carl Copeland lived in a sprawling home on the eastern side of Drakes Creek. While not as impressive as Big Jim's mansion, it was impressive nonetheless. A young black woman answered Gray's knock at the front door.

"Yes, sir?" she asked. She had a very slight Jamaican accent.

Gray held up his badge. "Nashville Police, here to see Mr. Copeland."

She stepped to the side so they could enter the house. "Oh, yes, sir. He's expecting you. Follow me, please."

Where Big Jim's house had been decorated tastefully and expensively -Gray had a feeling it was the work of the first Mrs. Diamante, not the second - Cowboy Carl's place had clearly been designed for comfort. They walked past a family room filled with overstuffed chairs and sofas accented with funky-colored pillows, several game systems, and the biggest television either of the detectives had ever seen. Here, too, multiple pictures and awards lined the walls, although not as many as at the crime scene. They followed the maid through a huge, sunny kitchen and out onto an enormous deck that provided a panoramic view of the water. Two jet skis zipped by, leaving frothy wakes behind them. Down below, on a vast expanse of lawn, a young woman sat at a picnic table reading while two small children played on a swing set. A man sat with his back to the house, watching them.

"Mr. Carl?" the maid said softly. "The detectives are here."

Cowboy Carl stood up and turned to face them. He looked to be in his mid-to-late- seventies, but he was clearly a man who took very good care of himself. He was trim and tanned and, when he shook with the detectives, his grip was firm. Beneath his cowboy hat, his eyes were clear and bright blue.

"Thank you, Louise," he said with a nod and a smile. He gestured to some chairs on the deck. "Have a seat, gentlemen," he said. Gray and Kennedy, who had introduced themselves when they shook hands, sat down.

"Nice view," Kennedy observed.

Copeland smiled. "It is, isn't it? I love to sit out here and watch the kids play."

"Your grandkids?" Gray asked.

Copeland laughed heartily. "Hell, no," he said. "My kids. That's my wife down there with them." Kennedy and Gray exchanged a surprised glance. The woman down on the lawn looked to be no more than thirty. Gray smiled and shook his head. *These old guys do pretty well for themselves*, he chuckled to himself. Kennedy took out his notebook and pen.

"So why don't you tell us what you heard," Gray

said. Cowboy Carl tipped his hat back on his head and told the detectives that he had called Big Jim to discuss what he would only call 'a private matter'. He said they were in the midst of their conversation when Jim started speaking to someone who had entered his office.

"What did he say?" Gray asked, leaning forward, his hands on his knees.

"First he said, 'I'm surprised to see you here,' or something close to that, then he said, 'You don't want to do that.' Then I think he either put the phone down or was holding it against his chest because it got very muffled.

"Do you know who he was talking to?"

"No, like I said, it was muffled. I couldn't make out anything the other person said, really. They were going at it pretty good, though, I'll tell you that."

"Could you tell anything about the other voice? Male, female?"

"No, sorry. I got tired of listening to them, and I hung up. Just as I did, though, I heard something, kind of a popping sound. I thought it was just the connection, but then I read that someone shot him. I think that must be what I heard." He shook his head sadly. "What a damn shame. This is a big loss for the business, I'll tell you what."

"Do you know exactly what time this was?" Gray asked.

"I can find out," Cowboy Carl said and stood up. "Let me get my phone." He disappeared into the house. When he came back out, he was holding the phone and scrolling. "Right here," he said, looking up at them. He turned the phone around and held it up to Gray. "Five-forty. We had talked for eight minutes before I hung up, so..."

"So you were on the phone with him from twenty to six and you disconnected eight minutes later. How long did you listen to the two of them argue?"

"Oh, not long, maybe twenty, thirty seconds. It could have been a little longer, I guess."

Gray did the math. "And the nine-one-one call came in at six-oh-two." He looked at Kennedy. "So whoever was in the office is probably the shooter." He looked at Copeland. "You couldn't recognize the voice?" Cowboy Carl shook his head. "And he never said a name?" Gray pressed.

"Nope, sorry."

"No, don't be. You've been a big help," Gray assured him.

As Copeland walked them out the front door and toward their car, he seemed to be deep in thought. Just before they all said goodbye, he took off his cowboy hat and scratched his head, then squinted at the sky.

"Something wrong?" Gray asked.

Copeland rubbed his chin with the back of the hand holding the hat, then set it back on his head. "Well, now, I don't want to say nothing that could get someone in Dutch 'cause, you know, I really don't know who was in Jim's office that day," he said.

"Why don't you tell us what you're thinking and we'll look into it?" Gray suggested.

"Well," Cowboy Carl said with a grim expression, "I can't be sure..."

"If you have someone in mind, let us worry about whether or not you're right." Kennedy said, trying to get the old man to give up a name.

"Well, Jim was in a foul mood that day. I talked to him three times, and he seemed more ticked off each time."

"Did he tell you what he was angry about?" Gray asked.

"One of his writers blew off a writing session with one of the hottest writers in town. Jim was going to fire him, like as not. But, I got the impression he was talking to a woman, and the writer's a guy." Kennedy closed the notebook and slipped it into his pocket. Then all three men shook hands.

"Thank you, Mr. Copeland," Gray said. "You've been a big help. I do have one more question, though, if you don't mind."

"Shoot," Copeland said, then immediately held up his hands. "Sorry, poor choice of words. What's your question, Detective?"

"Why didn't you call nine one one?"

Copeland rubbed his chin again. "Like I said, the sound was muffled and I was hanging up when I heard the pops. I just thought the connection was bad. I wish I *had* called. Maybe you would have caught the bastard."

FIFTEEN

Since they had already met the trophy wife, the detectives decided to pay a visit to the original Mrs. Diamante, Marjorie. She lived in the same house where Big Jim had started Diamond in the Rough over forty years earlier. When they'd built the house in Belle Meade, they'd hung onto this one in the hope their daughter would move back to Nashville eventually. Since that hadn't happened yet, once she and Jim divorced, she'd moved back in. The house was nothing compared to the mansion outside of town, but Marjorie liked this place better. It's where she and Jim had been happiest.

The small brick house, about two blocks from the

current location of the publishing company, sat on a beautifully manicured, postage stamp-sized lot that looked as if it had come straight from the pages of a gardening magazine. The detectives walked up a herringbone-patterned brick path that was surrounded on both sides by an extravagance of flowers.

Marjorie was a gracious host despite her loss; apparently she and Jim had remained quite close since he had jettisoned her to make room for Beverly. The first Mrs. Diamante served them fresh-squeezed lemonade and homemade cookies and showed them photo albums that chronicled Jim's meteoric rise to stardom in the late fifties and early sixties. A couple of the pictures were either the same or very similar to some of the ones in Jim's office. After they had observed the amenities, Gray got down to business.

"Mrs. Diamante..."

"Oh, please, call me Margie," the woman insisted.

Gray smiled. "Okay, Margie. We have some suspects in the case, but, to be perfectly honest, no one's jumping up and saying, 'Here I am!' We could use some help."

"Of course," Margie said. "Anything I can do."

"Well, first off, can you think of anyone who might have wanted to hurt your hus...Mr. Diamante?"

Margie laughed softly. "I'm sorry," she said, noticing their expressions. "It's just that, the music business can be very cutthroat and Jim won more battles than he lost. There were plenty of hard feelings. If that's the criteria, I'm afraid you're going to have quite an extensive list."

"Anyone stand out more than the others?" Kennedy asked.

Margie's brow furrowed. "Well, let's see," she said. "There was something just recently with a producer who accused Jim of stealing a song. It was nonsense, of course."

Gray looked surprised. "He kept you in the loop about the business?" he asked.

"He had no choice," Margie replied. "I own it."

"You mean since he passed? It goes to you?"

"No, I've owned it outright for a couple years. Technically, Jim worked for me." She smiled at their confused expressions. "Jim and I weren't married anymore, but Beverly didn't get a part of Diamond. Before he married her, he put everything in my name so she couldn't try to get her hooks in it."

"Your breakup sounds more amicable than most I've come across," Gray ventured. "And practical."

"For almost two years," Margie explained, "Beverly was the other woman. Finally, I grew tired of it and threw him out. Six months after they married, *I* became the other woman. Our relationship was better then than it had been during the last few years of our marriage. She may have looked better on his arm at the awards shows, but she didn't know him like I did."

"So to keep the business from her, he gave it to you?"

"Yes. But, it also helped when he ran into issues like this producer. Even if he had a case, the business would have been protected in the event of a lawsuit."

"I'm not sure that's how it works," Kennedy said, glancing up from his notebook.

"According to our lawyer it is," Margie countered. Kennedy jotted something down.

"May I ask who your lawyer is?" Gray asked.

"Neal Grimm."

"Okay. So what was the problem with the producer? He accused Jim of stealing a song?"

"Yes."

"I'm sorry to have to ask," Gray began, "but was there any truth to it?"

"No, absolutely not," Margie answered, sitting up straighter in her chair. Her eyes flashed with anger, causing Gray to backpedal.

"I don't mean to suggest anything, I just have to ask the question," he said. "I'm sorry if I've offended you."

Margie relaxed visibly. "No, no, it's all right. I know you're just doing your job."

"Thank you," Gray said, looking relieved. "Who was it that accused him?"

Margie looked away, then back at Gray and said, with distaste, "Cowboy Carl Copeland."

On the way back to the station, Gray looked over his partner's notes.

"I guess we can take Cowboy Carl off the list," Kennedy said. "Motive but no opportunity."

Gray made a grunting sound and looked up. "How do you figure?" he asked.

"Because he was on the phone with Jim when he got shot. The luds proved that."

"Okay, so they were on the phone. Gray didn't say anymore, just watched the younger detective, waiting to see if anything clicked. Suddenly, it was as if a light bulb went on over Kennedy's head and he smacked his forehead with his palm.

"Shit!" he exclaimed. "He was talking to him on

his cell. I'll find out which towers he was in range of. So for all we know, he *was* the shooter. This other voice might be a smokescreen."

"You're learning," Gray said.

"Although…Jeez, Henry, don't you think that's a little far-fetched? That he shot him while they were on the phone?"

"More far-fetched than a guy giving his business to his first wife, so his second wife gets left out in the cold, then having an affair with the first wife?"

Kennedy laughed. "Point taken."

"Anyway, the time of death can't be pinned down to the minute. Who's to say they really were on the phone when the shooting went down?"

Kennedy put on his blinker and moved into the right lane.

"Where to?" Gray asked.

"I need a coffee." He pulled into the parking lot of a Starbucks, found a spot, and shut the car off. "You want anything?"

"Nah, I'm not paying seven bucks for a cup of joe," he said, causing Kennedy to break out laughing.

"Man, you're cheap!" he exclaimed. "It's only four and, besides, I'm buying."

"Fine," Gray replied. "Nothing fancy, okay? Small, black, one Sweet and Low."

"Wild man," Kennedy joked and slammed the door. Gray went back to the notes, flipping back to the beginning of the case to see what he was missing. They were getting some information, but very little of it seemed connected in any way.

SIXTEEN

Later that afternoon, Gray was getting a Coke out of the machine in the hallway outside the squad room when a uniformed officer walked by him.

"Detective," the officer said as he walked past.

Gray looked up. "Hey, Ziele. How you doing?"

Officer Ziele stopped. "I'm good. You? How's your case coming?"

"Plenty of possible leads, but nothing's panned out yet. Hey, were you the first one on the scene or was it McKenzie?"

"We got there about the same time," Ziele said. "Mack went in first, but I was right behind him."

"And the outside door was open?"

"Yeah, all the way, like somebody pushed it hard on their way out. There were fresh chips in the side of the building where the knob hit it."

"Okay," Gray said. "And just the El Camino in the lot, right?" Ziele nodded. "No other vehicles, nothing on the street? Pedestrians?"

"Uh, yeah, one vehicle driving on Edgehill." He pulled out a steno book and flipped through it. "A black or dark blue van was going in the direction of Rose Park, make and model indeterminate."

"Did anyone run that down?" Gray asked.

"I sent the third unit to look for it, but no luck."

"Who was that?"

"Davis."

When Gray didn't respond, Ziele asked, "Everything all right?" Gray shook his head as if to clear it, then patted the other officer on the shoulder.

"Yeah, everything's fine. Thanks, Mike."

"No problem," Ziele said and walked away.

"Mike," Gray called after him. Ziele stopped walking and turned back to him, a hopeful expression on his face. "Do me a favor? Run over to the SunTrust branch near the scene and see if they have any security cameras facing the street."

Ziele nodded enthusiastically. "You got it, Detetive." It wasn't a secret in the department that Patrolman Ziele wanted his gold shield, and Gray knew if he used him on this case it would help him out. He figured it was a win-win: Mike Ziele was a good man.

He took the soda can out of the machine and placed it against his forehead, where a headache had started to bloom.

"That's not how those things work." Gray turned to see his captain walking toward him.

"I tried to drink it, but nothing came out," Gray responded.

The captain pointed. "See that little tab there? You need to pop that open."

"Oh," the detective cracked. "Is that how this works? Thanks, Captain. I don't know what we'd do without you."

"Are we going to be doing it without *you* soon?" the captain asked, his facetious tone gone.

Gray took his time before answering. "To be honest, I haven't decided yet."

"Well, you know we'd love to have you around for another twenty or thirty years."

Gray laughed. "Let's hope this case is solved by then."

"Problems?"

Gray shrugged. "I don't know. A lot of promising leads that don't seem to go anywhere. Ziele just gave me a new one, so I sent him to check it out."

"Okay," Paulson said. "Fill me in on what's going on." While they were talking, they had walked to Gray's desk. Kennedy was sitting at his, which sat pushed face-to-face up against his partner's, with a series of index cards spread across the surface. Gray looked at this and shook his head.

"All we know for certain," he began, "is that someone apparently surprised the victim in his office and shot him six times. Likewise, we're pretty sure that he was on the phone when he was shot. And this guy Wheeler discovered the body after the shooting and called nine-one-one, but how long after? That, we don't know.

"Right now I've got Ziele trying to track down a dark-colored van that was in the vicinity just before he and Mack got there. I sent him over to SunTrust to see if there's any security footage that might show it. So, someone shoots Big Jim while he's talking on the phone. Then Wheeler walks in after he's dead, calls us and leaves. Our guys get there. Then this guy, Carlisle, shows up. What the hell? The whole thing would have to be better choreographed than the Rockettes. How could this many people come and go in such a short amount of time, and all miss each other?"

"Unless Wheeler was the shooter," Kennedy added.

"Could be," Gray said, "This guy Copeland we went out to talk to says he heard the vic talking to someone who came into the office., but who knows? He's not sure, but he thinks it might have been a woman. But then Wheeler's voice isn't deep at all. When we were talking to the first wife and asked her who Big Jim might have had problems with, what name does she spit out but Copeland." Gray stroked his chin.

"I think your next move is to bring Wheeler in again," Paulson said. "You may not think he's the shooter, but maybe he saw someone leaving when he got there and forgot. Or maybe he's trying to protect somebody. Especially a woman."

"He didn't say anything if he did," Kennedy said. "I know if I were going to get jammed up on a murder charge, I'd mention everybody I saw that day and the three days before."

Paulson smiled, then said, "Well, it doesn't sound like you have anything better at the moment."

"Right," Kennedy said, getting up from the desk.

Once outside, Kennedy pointed the car toward JT's apartment on Elmhurst. Pulling into the parking lot, they were both relieved to see the old truck parked in front of his unit. The last thing they wanted right now was to have to go hunting for him. Gray strode to the door and knocked. When he didn't get a response, he knocked again, harder.

"JT Wheeler, it's Detective Gray. Answer the door, please." Two doors down, an elderly woman poked her head out of another apartment. Her skin was the color of fresh asphalt, her white hair was wound tightly around small rollers, and she was wearing a housecoat like Gray remembered his mother wearing back in the early sixties. There was a lit cigarette dangling from her lower lip. Unfiltered, he noticed.

"You're wasting your time," she called, blowing out twin jets of smoke through her nose.

"Ma'am?" Gray asked.

"If you're looking for JT, he's gone."

"What do you mean, 'gone'?" Gray asked, walking quickly toward her. "His truck's right there. Gone where?"

"He's taking the bus back home," she explained.

"How do you know that?" Gray demanded.

"On account of my husband drove him to the station. Oh," she said, squinting through the smoke, "here he is now." A dusty, bottle green Cadillac was coming into the parking lot like a cruise ship approaching a dock. It swung slowly toward the building and slid into a handicapped spot, taking half of another one in the process. A bald man squinted through the steering wheel as he pulled to a stop, then began his slow exit from the car. His eyes widened when he saw the two men in suits hurrying toward him.

"Did you give JT Wheeler a ride to the bus station?" Gray asked. The man nodded. "Where was he heading?"

"He said home, wherever that is," the man replied in a gravelly voice.

"Do you know what time the bus was?"

The man shook his head. "He didn't say the time, but I knew he had about a half hour wait after I dropped him off."

"How long ago?"

The man studied his watch. "Twenty minutes, give or take." Gray and Kennedy ran back to their car.

"Thanks," Kennedy called over his shoulder to the man.

"We're gonna need these," Gray said, flipping the two toggle switches on the dashboard that activated the lights and sirens. Then he grabbed the dashboard mic to alert any cars in the vicinity of the bus station to head over there. Ahead of them, cars scattered as Kennedy pushed theirs up to sixty-five miles per hour, then seventy. They made the trip from the apartment building to the Greyhound station on 5th Avenue South in about five minutes but, when they arrived, all the bus bays were empty. Kennedy pulled in, tires squealing, eliciting surprised looks from several people standing there with everything from matched sets of luggage to paper shopping bags.

"Shoot!" Kennedy exclaimed, hitting the steering wheel in frustration. "Now what?"

"Now we go inside and figure out which bus he's

on and how long ago it left," Gray said as he opened the car door. An elderly man in blue coveralls was pushing a broom outside the station doors.

"Hey, can't park there," he called, walking toward them, ready to challenge. "Can't you read?" He gestured with the head of the broom to a faded sign that read 'Busses Only' and featured the familiar blue and grey dog logo."

Gray flipped open his badge wallet as he rushed past him. "Metro Police," he barked and the janitor stood down.

SEVENTEEN

As soon as Gray ran back out of the station, they headed toward the interstate. Kennedy raced up the on-ramp onto Route 40 eastbound, lights flashing and siren wailing. Eight miles out of downtown, just before the airport exit, they spotted three Highway Patrol vehicles stopped along the side of the road with their lights flashing, lined up behind a Greyhound bus. He pulled up behind them, and the detecctives rushed to the bus and boarded. Halfway toward the rear on the right, JT Wheeler was watching them, terrified.

Gray strode back to him as the other passengers stared. "Going somewhere, JT?" Gray asked. "Come on, get up." JT stood up and Gray grabbed him roughly by the arm. "You got a bag or anything?"

JT motioned to the seat next to his. "That's mine," he said, his mouth desert-dry.

"Anything else?"

"Under the bus," he said. Gray dragged him down the aisle and led him down the steps and onto the shoulder of the road.

"We need his bag," he said to the confused-looking driver, who was watching the drama unfold, wide-eyed and was already looking forward to relating this story to his wife over dinner. He got off the bus and walked along the side while curious riders pressed their noses against the windows above, opened the baggage door, and looked expectantly at JT.

"The brown one with the black tag," JT told him. The driver reached in and pulled it out and Kennedy carried it back to the car with his other bag. He put them in the trunk and walked back to where Gray and JT were, grabbed JT by the arm, and led him to the car. He put him in the back seat, then got behind the wheel while Gray was shaking hands with the State Troopers. He walked back to the car and slid in, then turned to look at their passenger.

"Didn't we tell you to stay in town, JT? Taking off was a dumb move, my friend." Kennedy merged into traffic, tooted at the staties, and took the airport exit. He worked his way over to Donelson Pike and jumped on Route 41 West heading back to the city. JT slumped in the back seat, staring out the window silently. Gray and Kennedy talked about the Titans' chances in the upcoming football season and about Vanderbilt basketball, then about taking a bike trip some weekend north to Guthrie, Kentucky, where

Gray's former partner, Lonnie Bergen lived. Gray enjoyed these trips, but since he and his wife split up, he always felt like a third wheel. Kennedy's wife, Jodie, was always along, as had been Priscilla. Now, Gray thought maybe he'd ask a woman friend in the coroner's office if she'd be interested in going along. There was no denying the chemistry between them, so why not? He thought. Besides, she and Lonnie had been friends when he was on the job, which lessened the 'date' aspect of her joining them.

The detectives and JT were sitting in a cramped interrogation room.

"Why'd you take off, JT?" Kennedy asked.

"I didn't take off," JT mumbled. "I just wanted to spend some time back home." Neither detective responded. When the silence in the room started to feel suffocating, JT said, "I think I want a lawyer." The detectives exchanged a knowing glance.

"That's fine, JT," Gray said evenly. "A guilty man *should* have a lawyer."

JT's eyes flew open wide, and he sat up ramrod straight. "I'm not guilty of anything!" he said, placing both hands on the table as if he were about to launch himself at one or both of them. Kennedy immediately stood up.

"Easy, JT," he said. "Don't do anything you'll regret." JT slumped back in his seat.

"I'm not, but I didn't do anything. I'm not guilty of anything."

"Then why do you need a lawyer?" Gray asked in that same calm tone.

"'Cause you guys are trying to railroad me."

"Railroad you?" Gray burst out laughing. "This isn't some two-bit spaghetti western, JT. Nobody's trying to 'railroad' you. And, just so you know, in my thirty years on the job, you're the first person who's ever used the term 'railroad me' in my presence."

JT looked put-out. "So you think making me feel stupid is going to get me to open up to you?" Gray was a little taken aback by JT's abrupt change in demeanor.

"Wow, feeling a little ballsy all of a sudden?" he asked in a tone that almost sounded admiring. "What exactly is it you have to open up *about*, JT?" Gray leaned closer, trying to intimidate the young man. It worked. JT leaned as far away from him as he could, to the point where the front legs of his chair came up off the floor.

"I've got nothing to say," JT sulked, folding his arms across his chest and turning his head to the side.

Gray turned to Kennedy. "You believe this guy?" he asked, hands outstretched, palms toward the ceiling.

"Why don't you take a walk?" Kennedy suggested, his signal to Gray that it was time for 'good cop' to take over. He found it hard to believe that this tactic could really work, but it usually did. Gray looked at him for a long second, then shrugged.

"I'm going to get a Coke. You want anything?" He purposely didn't say anything to JT so Kennedy would be the one to offer him a drink.

"How about you, JT?" Kennedy asked, friendly. "You want a cold drink?" JT stared at him for a moment, then nodded. "Great, what would you like? We have Coke, Diet, Orange…"

"Orange," JT said. Gray was watching him, but JT was careful to avoid his gaze. "Thank you," he said to Kennedy. Gray left the room.

"Now, JT," Kennedy began, "we've got quite a conundrum here. You know what that is, right?"

"A problem," JT ventured.

"That's close," Kennedy praised, suddenly JT's new best friend. "But it's actually more like a puzzle. And, believe me, this case *is* a puzzle. To be honest, I'd just like to ask you some questions so we can clear you. Would that be alright?" Before JT could answer, he added, "Now if you still want that lawyer, that's fine. But I have to be honest with you, things are going go a lot smoother for you if you just talk to me. You say you didn't do anything, so why not just clear it up now, and you can go on your way?"

"What about my bus ticket?" JT asked.

"What about it?"

"I'm out a hundred and sixty bucks because you guys pulled me off. What about that?"

"Don't worry about it. Once we clear this up, I'll personally put you on a bus even if I have to pay for the ticket myself." He waited thirty seconds while JT thought it over. "What do you say? Deal?" JT nodded. "Okay, good," Kennedy said. "So let's go back to the day Big Jim was killed…"

JT went over the story again, starting with how he'd blown off an important writing appointment to spend the afternoon with another man's wife, how he'd stopped at the overlook above the city; everything up to and including finding his boss's body. In the middle of the retelling, Gray came back with the drinks, but he let Kennedy handle the entire interview.

After an hour, the detectives decided to take a break. They left JT in the interview room and went out into the hallway.

"What do you think?" Gray asked. "You think he's good for it?"

"I don't know," Kennedy said thoughtfully. "I mean, I didn't think there was a chance until he skipped town. Tell you what, though. If he didn't do it, he's got the worst luck in the world."

"You got that right," Gray agreed. "We still don't have a gun. Whoever the shooter is, he must have tossed it."

"I'll get some uniforms out there to canvass," Kennedy said. "Mike," he called to Officer Ziele, who was standing nearby. "I'll be right back; then I need you to come with me. We're close to arresting this kid, but we need to find the murder weapon." He turned back to Gray. "How many guys should I send out?"

"I'd say six," Gray said, "but run it by the captain first, so that he's in the loop. Let's get a warrant for his apartment, too, just in case he wasn't smart enough to get rid of it."

"Will do," Kennedy agreed."

He walked away, and Gray looked at Ziele. "Find us a gun, Mike. It would look awfully good in your jacket." he said. Ziele smiled, and Gray walked into the room where JT was. JT stared at him, clearly upset, as one would expect under the circumstances. Gray knew just from observing his body language that he expected to be placed under arrest, so his words were clearly a surprise.

"You're free to go, JT."

Relief flooded JT's pale face. "So you believe

me?"

Gray shook his head, and JT sagged. "Personally, I don't, but we don't have enough to arrest you yet. I can assure you though it's only a matter of time."

EIGHTEEN

The young women, both dressed in formal maid attire, were standing at the bottom of the impressive central staircase, giggling and whispering. Upstairs, they could hear loud grunts, moans, and the occasional sound of something -or someone- banging into a wall with a great deal of force. They were so mesmerized by what they were hearing that neither of them was aware that the front door had opened and a young woman, probably around the same age as them, as a matter of fact, stood staring daggers at their backs. When she spoke -quite sharply- the smiles fell from their faces, and they spun around, mortified.

"What, exactly, are you two doing?" the young

woman demanded. Before she finished the sentence, though, she realized the answer on her own. Her eyes moved up the stairs as the moaning grew louder, then stopped suddenly. Less than a minute later, a young man came down the stairs, carrying a worn pair of work boots. His eyes widened at the sight of the new arrival, and he ducked his head in embarrassment.

"Ma'am," he mumbled, turning sideways to squeeze by the three woman. As he went, his stocking feet slipped on the marble, but he regained his balance. The one he had addressed turned to watch him go into the kitchen and, presumably, out of the house, and then turned her attention back to the maids, who seemed fascinated by the goings-on.

"Don't you have anything to do?" she asked, her tone intimating that, if they didn't find something -and fast- they'd be job-hunting by the end of the day.

"Yes, ma'am," one of them said, and they scurried away in opposite directions. The young woman turned her attention back to the stairs, where her father's second wife, Beverly, was making her grand entrance.

"Well, well, look who's here. So lovely to see you, Lacey." She walked up to her and attempted to plant a kiss on her cheek, but Lacey turned away.

"My father's not even in the ground yet and you're already entertaining the help, Beverly?"

"Au contraire, Lacey," Beverly said, "it was I who was being entertained. My young friend is so…energetic."

You're a pig," Lacey retorted. "I can't imagine what Daddy ever saw in you."

Beverly stepped back and waved her hand in front of herself like a game show model showing off a new car. "Take a look, darling," she said. "Maybe you can figure it out.

"So did you kill him yourself or did one of your boyfriends do it?" Lacey asked. If she'd initially had any intent of trying to conceal her hostility for her father's wife, that ship had sailed.

Beverly shook her head. "Poor Lacey, still laboring under the delusion that your father was some wonderful man. Believe me, little girl, the cops have more suspects than Carter has pills. Everybody hated him."

"Go to hell, you condescending bitch." Beverly looked like she was about to respond, and Lacey took a step closer to her. "And if you ever call me 'little girl' again, I'll slap that smug expression clean off your stupid face."

Beverly's smirk became even more pronounced. "Oh, Lacey, Lacey, Lacey. I'll tell you what, sweetheart. You leave my house right now, and I won't call the police and have them drag you out. How's that sound?"

Lacey stepped even closer, so they were nose-to-nose. "Listen to me, you whore." Beverly's smile winked out like a candle in the wind. "I'm not going anywhere. If anyone's leaving, it's you."

Beverly took a step back. "This is *my* home," she said through gritted teeth. "I am certainly not leaving *my* home." She was careful to make sure Lacey heard the emphasis she placed on the word 'my'.

"Wait until they connect you to the murder," Lacey responded, going for the kill shot. "Your home will be a place with striped sunlight."

"Why, you little bitch," Beverly sputtered. "I

ought to..." She balled up her fist but left her hand dangling at her side. Lacey, who had been a two-sport athlete at the University of Tennessee, saw this and smiled.

"Go ahead, Bev, take your best shot."

Beverly returned her smile, but it didn't reach her eyes. "No, I think not," she said. "I don't want to tangle with someone like you." Lacey's smile faltered slightly, and she watched Beverly warily, head cocked, waiting for the inevitable. "After all, I know how rough and tough you softball players can be. Or are you a lady golfer now?" She batted her eyes as Lacey seethed. She knew full well this kind of a cheap shot was to be expected when one spoke to Beverly, but it got under her skin, just the same. And Beverly knew it. Lacey was about to respond when a door opened and shut, and the sound of someone walking rapidly towards them filled the room, heels clicking on the marble floor.

"Ladies!" a stern voice called out. They both turned to see Phillip, Big Jim's long-time man Friday. He was a slight, unassuming black gentleman who, despite his small stature, commanded a great deal of respect, not only from the other help, but from his employers, as well. He quickly closed the gap between himself and the two women, his salt-and-pepper, close-trimmed hair all but shooting sparks, dark eyes flashing. "This is hardly the time or the place."

"*Excuse me?*" Beverly demanded. Phillip didn't back down, however; if anything, he stood taller.

"What would Mr. Diamante say about this kind of behavior?" he asked, then stared an unspoken challenge at Beverly, who averted her eyes. Phillip turned to

Lacey. "Hello, Miss Lacey," he said warmly, reaching for the suitcase she had carried in. "Shall I bring this up to your room?"

Lacey, who seemed a bit distracted, tore her eyes away from Beverly and looked at Phillip.

"Oh, no, thank you, Phillip. I think I'll go check into a hotel." She sniffed the air theatrically. "It smells like a French whorehouse in here." Phillip looked at the floor so Beverly wouldn't see him smiling, but her eyes were locked onto Lacey anyway.

"Good idea," Beverly said. "I think there's a gay and lesbian flophouse downtown." Phillip slipped between the two women, just in case, then turned to Lacey.

"How's Dr. David these days, Miss Lacey?" Dr. David Brown was Lacey's fiancé.

Lacey smiled at him. "He's well, Phillip, thank you for asking." She favored Beverly with an innocent smile, then turned abruptly and made a beeline toward the front door. Phillip caught up to her and reached for the bag again.

"I'll be more than happy to take this for you," he said. This time she let go of the handle, and they walked out to the driveway where her car was parked.

Once they reached it, Lacey turned to him and took his hand. "Phillip, when I got here, she was upstairs with one of the hands. I think his name is Brock." She wrinkled her nose in distaste. "We haven't even had the funeral yet."

Phillip squeezed her hand and frowned. "I'll take care of it," he assured her.

Lacey looked alarmed. "Don't fire him," she said.

"Please. I blame her, not him. Just put an end to it." Phillip looked at her closely; then his face softened.

"Alright, Miss Lacey. As you wish. I'll talk to him." Lacey suddenly leaned forward and kissed him on the cheek.

"Thank you, Phillip," she said. Ordinarily, that would be considered by some to be a breach of etiquette, but they had known each other Lacey's whole life and to her Phillip was more like a favorite uncle than a member of the staff.

Phillip smiled. "It's not hard to see why you had your father wrapped around your little finger," he said, opening her car door for her. Now, his smile faded. "I'm truly sorry for your loss, Miss Lacey."

She hugged him, hard. "I know, Phillip. Thank you." He waved as she drove off, then turned to see Beverly standing at an upstairs window, watching them, her lovely face twisted with anger.

Phillip fought a sudden, sophomoric urge to flip her off. "Bitch," he muttered under his breath. He returned to the house, knowing that his days of working there were numbered. *Let her fire me*, he thought, secure in the knowledge that, over the years, Big Jim had made provisions to ensure that Phillip would live quite comfortably should he ever choose to retire. He walked back into the foyer whistling under his breath.

NINETEEN

"You know," Gray said, leaning back in his chair, "there's this bar downtown called Sonny's Place. Run by a guy named Munson. I think you should go have a talk with him."

"Why?" Kennedy asked. "What's he got to do with this?"

"Nothing directly, but he's got his ear to the ground. I've gotten some good intel from him in the past."

"So if you have a relationship with the guy, why am I going by myself?"

Gray smiled. "We had, um, a run-in, you might say. Couple years back."

Kennedy's curiosity was piqued. "Oh?"

Gray laughed and shook his head. "Suffice it to say, he won't talk to me anymore."

"Uh huh."

Gray laughed again. "Don't worry, he's got full use of that arm again." Kennedy shook his head. "Pretty much. Glad you asked, kid?"

"Not really," Kennedy replied.

As soon as he walked into the bar, Kennedy had to take off his glasses, which had darkened in the sunlight and now were too dark for the shadowy room. A few cowboy types at the bar looked up at the newcomer in the suit, then turned back to their drinks. There were a few empty pool tables under Tiffany-style lamps advertising various beer brands, and a couple of pinball machines, along with the requisite autographed pictures of NASCAR drivers and monster trucks adorning the dark-paneled walls. The billiard lamps hanging over the tables were all off, but an old Wurlitzer jukebox tucked in a back corner was belting out a Hank Williams Jr. song. He waited a few seconds for his eyes to adjust completely, then weaved his way through a handful of tables to the end of the bar. The bartender glanced up at him, then quickly looked away and went back to wiping glasses. Kennedy knocked on the counter. The bartender looked up again - reluctantly- then finally threw the bar towel over his shoulder and approached him.

"Help ya?" he asked. His tone indicated he would rather be doing pretty much anything *but* helping him. Undergoing a root canal, perhaps. When Kennedy reached for his badge, the barkeep waved him off. "No need to flash your tin," he said with a grimace. "I made you the second you came through the door."

Kennedy smiled. "Okay. You want to tell me why I'm here, too?"

"Big Jim, right?"

"You're good," Kennedy chuckled. "You got the Hot Lotto numbers for Wednesday while we're at it?"

"If I had them, you think I'd be standing here with a dirty towel draped over my shoulder?" the bartender grumbled.

"So what's the word on Big Jim?" Kennedy asked. "People must be talking about it."

"People have their opinions," the man offered cautiously. "Why are you coming to me, anyway? What makes you think I know anything?"

Kennedy pulled out his notebook, causing the bartender to throw a quick glance at his patrons. One of the men at the bar saw him and lifted an empty glass. "'Scuse me," the barkeep said. "I'll be right back." Kennedy tapped his pen on the bar and waited.

"Let's start with your name," he said when the man returned.

"Mike, but everyone calls me Sonny. So you didn't answer my question; why me?"

Kennedy had been warned about this. "Henry Gray sends his regards," he said. "You got a last name, Mike?"

"Jesus Christ!" the bartender boomed, then glanced back at the barflies.

"Seriously?" Kennedy said, amused by the reaction Gray's name elicited. "Your last name is Jesus Christ? Is that one word or two?"

"Come on, don't bust my balls. I don't want

nothing to do with him.

"Yeah, he told me you'd feel that way. That's why I'm here."

"I don't have nothing to say," Mike said.

"Okay, that's fine. If you don't have nothing to say, you must have something to say, right" Kennedy replied, eliciting a bewildered look. "Now, what are you hearing?" When Mike didn't answer, Kennedy said, "Look, you can talk to me or talk to Detective Gray. It's your choice, but you're going to talk to one of us."

Mike put up his hands in a gesture of surrender. "Okay, okay. Maybe I heard that a couple of people in the business had some serious problems with Big Jim," he said.

"Oh, yeah? What kind of problems?"

"Hypnotically, you know?"

Kennedy was taken aback. "What?"

"Hypnochronically," Sonny said. "You know, like what if."

"Hypothetically?"

"Yeah, that's what I said. Hypothetically."

"Okay," Kennedy agreed, trying not to smile. "Hypnochronically."

Sonny glanced around the bar, but no one seemed to be paying them any attention. "Song stealing, for one."

"Who was that?"

"A girl named Dixie Lee Wrenn, two 'n's."

Kennedy looked up. "Seriously? Dixie Lee Wrenn?"

"Yep." Mike smiled, revealing a couple of gaps in his tobacco-stained teeth. "The Carolina Songbird."

He said this last with fondness. "Nice girl, Dixie. Jim screwed her over. In more ways than one, if you know what I mean." He tipped Kennedy a wink.

"So he had an affair with her?"

"Yeah, if you can call bending her over his desk whenever he got the urge an affair." As Kennedy wrote it down, a tall, lanky man suddenly stood up, glared at them, threw a few bills on the counter, then stalked out of the bar. They both watched him go; and then Kennedy turned back.

"Ah, hell's bells," Sonny said. "I forgot he was here."

"Who was that?"

"Rusty Sills. He's a songwriter and him and Dixie, you know."

"Okay. You said he screwed her over in more ways than one. What other ways did he screw her?" Sonny glanced back at his patrons again, then leaned forward and lowered his voice.

"No one can prove it, but the biggest hit to come out of Jim's company in the last five years was a song called "Slow Burnin' Love" by Arielle Fox. Ever hear it?"

Kennedy shook his head. "Not that I know of."

"It's a beautiful song, just gorgeous. It was Ari's first big hit. I mean, now she's a household name, but back then, nobody had ever heard of her." *I still haven't,* Kennedy thought. "That song made her who she is."

"What's this got to do with Jim?"

"Well, rumor is it was Dixie's song in the first place, but Jim pulled some funny business, and his name wound up on it as the writer. He produced it, too.

Ari Fox was his big discovery. They both got rich, and Dixie got squat. Well, Ari got rich, and Jim got richer."

"Do you think this Ari girl had anything to with it?"

"Nah, word is she's as pure as the driven snow. It was all on Big Jim. Everyone likes to think Big Jim was this gentle old man, watching over the business, and he could be just that. But he could be lower than a rattlesnake and twice as mean when he thought it was called for."

"So, who else had an ax to grind with my victim?" Munson mentioned a couple names, but quickly discounted them. "What about that guy, Sills?" Kennedy asked.

The bartender shook his head. "Nah, Rusty thought the sun shined out of Jim's ass."

"Even though he repeatedly raped his girlfriend?"

"I don't think Rusty's ever believed that," Munson said. "Besides, it could be just talk. It ain't like anybody saw it happen."

Kennedy closed the notebook and slid it into his pocket. "Thanks for your help. I'll tell Detective Gray you send him your kindest regards."

Munson grimaced and shook his head. "Don't bother. He wouldn't believe you anyway."

Kennedy went out to his car. When he opened the door, waves of hot air rolled out at him.

"Crap," he muttered. He reached in and started the car, turned the air conditioner up to full blast, then shut the door and went down the block to a little market for a cold drink. As he walked back out onto the hot sidewalk, someone who had been in the store followed him outside.

"Sure is a hot one," a male voice behind him said.

"Yep," he replied without turning around.

"You were asking about Big Jim and all in Sonny's."

Kennedy stopped and turned around to see the man who had left the bar a few minutes earlier. He paused with his Coke bottle halfway to his lips. "Yeah, I was," he said. "What about it?"

The man looked slightly uncomfortable, glancing around furtively. "I don't usually get involved in stuff, you know?" Kennedy waited patiently. "It's just that I heard Munson mention that Dixie Lee gal and I know there's no way she'd get involved in something like that."

"You do, huh?" Out came the notebook. The man glanced around again.

"That's all I know," he insisted, mopping at his brow with a blue bandanna. "You ain't gonna need that pad." Kennedy, who was very adept at reading body language, felt the man had more to say.

"I'll tell you what," Kennedy said. "My car's right down the block and the A/C is going full blast. How 'bout I give you a lift." The man looked at him uncertainly, then nodded. They walked to the car and got in. It had to be twenty degrees cooler in the car than outside. "Where to?" Kennedy asked. The man gave him an address, and he pulled into traffic.

"So, I'm thinking you have more to tell me," he said after a minute of silence.

The man took a deep breath. "I'll just say that Dixie wasn't the only person with an ax to grind when it come to Jim. Don't get me wrong, though, Jim was a great man and a great friend."

"What's your name?" Kennedy asked.

"Vernon Sills. But, everybody calls me Rusty." He reached a hand toward Kennedy, who looked at it in surprise, but then shook with him. In his experience, people never wanted to shake hands with cops. And, for obvious reasons, none of the cops he knew made a habit of shaking with civilians while on the job. As they drove, Kennedy asked a few casual questions, and Rusty was only too happy to answer them.

"So you're Miss Wrenn's boyfriend?" Kennedy asked finally.

Rusty eyed him carefully, then answered in measured tones, "You might say that," he allowed, "although, I think we're a little old for boyfriend, girlfriend." He pulled out a battered pack of Winstons. "You mind?" he asked.

"Sorry," Kennedy said, "The law says no smoking in any government building or vehicle."

"Right," Rusty said. "Right." He slipped the pack back into his pocket. "I'm telling you, officer, and not just because we're close: Dixie couldn't-a had nothing to do with Big Jim's death, may he rest in peace."

Kennedy glanced at him. "You were fond of Jim, huh?"

"He gave me my start when I came here from San Antone in the seventies. I loved him like a brother."

"Okay. And what about Miss Wrenn?"

Rusty took a long look out the window. Finally, he said, "I know she don't have it in her to do this."

"So, if you're saying that, is it safe to assume she didn't like him?"

Rusty looked at him, his blue eyes shining,

whether with tears or beers, Kennedy didn't know.

"Let's say he wasn't her favorite person in the business, but she ain't no murderer, neither. And we can leave it at that. This is me." Rusty pointed to a neat and tidy apartment building on their left and Kennedy pulled to the curb on front of a television repair shop. *Don't see many of those anymore,* he mused. He watched Rusty cross the street, then pulled away.

After dropping Rusty off, Kennedy drove back to the station to meet up with his partner, who had spent the morning in court testifying on another of their cases. He found him in the parking lot, chatting with an attractive female officer. When Gray saw him, he put his hand on the officer's arm and said something that made her laugh, then walked toward where Kennedy was pulling into a parking spot.

"What'd you find out?" he asked when he got within earshot. "Probably bupkis, right?"

Kennedy shook his head. "No, actually I got some interesting stuff." He pulled out his notebook and filled Gray in.

"You're right, that is interesting," Gray said.

"And what did you find out?" Kennedy asked with a grin, lifting his chin toward the officer Gray had been talking to, who glanced over at them then quickly looked away.

Gray fixed a stern gaze on his partner. "I found out that you're a nosy bastard," he said, then laughed.

TWENTY

A few days after JT had been pulled off the bus, an attorney showed up at the police station with an attractive blonde in tow and asked to see Detectives Gray and Kennedy.   He was ushered into an interrogation room, offered a cup of coffee, and told they'd be right with him. Five minutes later, the two detectives and Captain Paulson entered the room.

"I represent Justin Wheeler," the attorney, Matt Martin, began, "and Amanda Barrish." He tipped his head toward the blonde.   That got everybody's attention.

"You're a tough woman to track down," Gray said to her. "We've been looking for you."

Mindy Barrish appraised him coolly. "I was out of town," she said, tossing her long hair over her shoulder with a practiced gesture.

"Really?" Gray said, nodding. "And where were you?"

She started to answer, but the lawyer cut her off. "Mrs. Barrish is here as a cooperating witness. It's not necessary for her to divulge her travel itinerary to you."

"Okay," Gray said evenly. "Then why is she here?"

"She can corroborate Mr. Wheeler's alibi. They spent the afternoon together."

"Is that true?" Gray asked. She nodded. "Until what time?" She told him. Gray turned to Attorney Martin. "Just out of curiosity, Counselor, how long have you been Mrs. Barrish's attorney?

"For close to twenty years, not that it matters."

"And how long have you been representing Mr. Wheeler?"

The lawyer stood. "Are we done here, gentleman? I have an appointment."

The detectives were in Paulson's office, and JT's name had dropped way down on their suspect list. With Mindy Barrish providing an alibi, and without any viable evidence against him, there was no reason to continue looking at him.

"Maybe we shouldn't be so hasty," Kennedy said. "Even if he left when she said he did, he still had time to get into the city, kill Big Jim, and take off."

"Yeah," Gray said, "maybe, but don't forget what we already know. Jim was alive at five forty-eight, which is when Cowboy Carl claims to have heard noises as he was hanging up, so we'll assume that's when the shooting took place. Do we really think this kid Wheeler stuck around for fourteen minutes after shooting the guy, then called it in?"

"I think you need to move on," Paulson said. "Wheeler's not your man."

"I have to agree with you," Gray admitted.

"What about the wife?"

"What about her?" Gray shrugged. "We know she had everything to gain from Big Jim dying. Apparently, he was planning to divorce her, which meant she'd wind up with next to nothing, but Wall told us to back off. Well, let me rephrase that. First he told us to, 'treat her with kid gloves', I think, was the way he put it."

Kennedy nodded. "Word-for-word, but then he told us she should be our number one suspect."

"That's right," Gray interjected. "He was the first one to say Jim was going to dump her."

"Who was the second?" Paulson asked.

"Buddy Carlisle."

"And he is?"

"The guy who's worked with Jim almost from Day One."

"So, the chief told you to take it easy on her, and then he told you to look at her closely? Kind of mixed signals, huh?"

"We talked about that," Kennedy said. "What if he does want us to lay off, but once he said it, thought it sounded hinky to the other guys in the room. Like Major McAllister?"

"McAllister was there?"

Gray nodded, then shrugged. "What do you

think?" He was looking at Paulson from the corner of his eye.

Paulson looked at him, then held up his hands. "Now, hold on, Henry," he said. "The chief is not involved in this. There's no way in hell, so get that thought right out of your head."

"How can you be so sure?" Gray asked.

Paulson didn't answer him. "Who else is on your list?" he asked.

"Well, he had some well-known issues with Cowboy Carl Copeland," Kennedy said.

"Weren't they talking when it went down?"

"Yeah," Kennedy replied, "but the cowboy was on his cell, so he could have been anywhere. I'm waiting for the DA to subpoena the phone records so we can see what tower he was pinging off when they were on the phone.

Paulson frowned. "So you guys think he might have been at the office? I thought he heard Jim talking to someone?

"All we have is his word," Gray said.

"Alright," Paulson said, making a note, "I'll light a fire under the DA. Who else?"

"A woman named Dixie Lee Wrenn."

Paulson looked up quickly. "I know that name. They used to call her The Songbird or something like that."

"Yeah, the Carolina Songbird," Kennedy said.

"That's it," Paulson agreed. "What's her connection?"

"She worked with Big Jim a long time ago and, according to what my witness said, he sexually assaulted her repeatedly."

"Jesus Christ," Paulson said. "This guy had a reputation for being squeaky clean."

"To the public, yeah, but not in the business," Gray said.

"I was told that Jim produced a huge hit for a girl named..." -he consulted his notebook- "Arielle Fox and..."

"I've heard of her, too. She's huge right now," Paulson interrupted.

"Yeah, well, her first hit was supposedly written by Big Jim, but the rumor is he stole it from Dixie."

"What did Copeland say he heard again?"

Kennedy riffled some pages. "First Jim said, 'I'm surprised to see you here' and then, 'You don't want to do that."

"So it sounds like he knew whoever killed him. Go talk to Dixie Songbird."

TWENTY-ONE

When Rusty walked into Dixie Lee's apartment, she had been dozing, but now she was wide awake.

"What do you mean, they was asking about me?" Dixie Lee Wrenn was huddled on her couch, clutching a pillow, with her knees drawn up to her chest and a half box of Kleenex on the floor next to her. Her mascara had run down her cheeks in a flood of hot tears. "Why do they think I had anything to do with it?"

Rusty Sills sat down next to her and ran a hand over her back and shoulders. "Now, just you calm down, Dixie Lee. I told the cop you couldn't have had nothing to do with it." Under his breath he mumbled,

"Dammit, I knew I shouldn't have told her."

Dixie raised her head. "What?"

"Nothing," Rusty said. He continued rubbing her shoulders. "You got nothing to worry about."

"But, Rusty," she wailed.

"Shhh," Rusty whispered. "Why don't you close your eyes for a little bit?" After a while, Dixie's breathing became deep and rhythmic, and Rusty slid his arm out from under her head. He was glad because the amount of heat coming off her was like the heat coming off a skillet on the stove. Once free, he began to pace back and forth in the small apartment. Rusty had spent more than a few nights here over the years, but he and Dixie had never taken the next step and moved in together. Still, if he decided to stay the night, he had a change of clothes and a toothbrush. In all honesty, he wanted to go home but didn't feel comfortable leaving her alone.

Dixie Lee Wrenn, widely known as 'The Carolina Songbird', had first caught the attention of Big Jim Diamond twenty-five years ago when she and her mother arrived in Nashville, fresh from the family farm just outside of Gaffney, South Carolina. Dixie was a favorite on the county fair circuit in the Carolinas, belting out all the big hits from the traditional female Country stars of the sixties and seventies. Polly, her mom, thought her daughter needed to relocate to Music City to move her career along. Polly herself had spent some time there when she was young, rubbing shoulders with many of Country music's elite, including Big Jim Diamond. In fact, although Big Jim didn't know it, he was Dixie's father. And Polly thought this would be the perfect bargaining chip to force Jim to work with the girl and make her a star. *Lord knows we could use the money*, Polly often thought, not that it was a particularly accurate portrayal of their circumstances: The farm was actually quite successful. Nevertheless, she'd been planning this little 'surprise' for Jim for several years, pretty much since the day she realized Dixie could really sing.

Years after her dream of making it in the music business died on the vine when she discovered she was pregnant, Polly saw Dixie as her instrument, the vehicle that would right all the wrongs she'd faced in her life, real or imagined. Back when she was Polly June Baker, she'd moved to Nashville from Gaffney and hitched her wagon to Big Jim Diamond. All she'd gotten out of the ride, though, was a bun in the oven. When she skulked back to South Carolina, confused and afraid, she'd quickly married a slow-witted local boy named Tommy Wrenn, whose family just happened to own a large farm outside of town that boasted about forty percent of the local peach crop. There'd been other boys she would have preferred, but Tommy was the only one who was willing to raise another man's child. How his parents felt about the situation was a whole other story, but Tommy, for once in his life, had dug his heels in against them and gone ahead and married Polly. Four months later, when Dixie came along on an unusually cold and rainy March night, he'd accepted her as his own.

That was fourteen years before Polly decided the time was ripe to call in a favor. She kissed Tommy goodbye, packed Dixie in the car, and headed west, planning to make both Gaffney and Tommy Wrenn distant memories. During the whole, roughly six-hour drive, she talked incessantly about someone she called 'Uncle Jim', the man she swore was going to help her daughter become one of Nashville's brightest stars. Arriving in the city, she got a room at a small, drab motel, the cheapest one she could find; to save money that didn't really need saving. They brought their bags inside and set them down. Then Polly told Dixie to put on her best dress.

"Why, Mama?" Dixie asked.

Polly smiled. "Because we're going to see your Uncle Jim. You want to look pretty for him, don't you?"

"Yes, Mama," the girl answered dutifully, then changed into the blue dress she wore to church most Sundays.

At just fourteen years old, Dixie could have passed for twenty-two or three. She was about five-foot-three, with a profusion of blonde, curly hair surrounding an angelic face and bright blue eyes. As some girls tend to be at that age, she was quite well-developed. In all honesty, if she'd been taller she probably could have gone into modeling and had a long and successful career; she was that beautiful. But, it didn't matter. She loved writing and singing songs and, truth be told, Polly never considered any other options for her lovely daughter other than being a singing sensation. She imagined her someday bringing the crowd at The Grand Ol' Opry to their feet, their thunderous applause echoing through the old building. Every dream that Polly ever had for herself had turned into her plan for Dixie Lee.

TWENTY-TWO

Lacey Diamante was sitting by herself in the coffee shop of the Holiday Inn on West End Avenue in downtown Nashville when she happened to glance up and spot a familiar face. He appeared to have noticed her at the same moment, and now he was navigating his way through the crowded room.

"Lacey!" he said, seemingly happy to see her. "How are you?" Then his smile faded, and he reached for her hand. "I'm terribly sorry about Big Jim. He'll be sorely missed."

"Thank you," Lacey said. "It's kind of you to say that, Mr. Copeland."

"Well, it's the truth. And call me Carl." He

pulled out the chair opposite hers and started to sit down, and then stopped. "May I?" he asked, bushy eyebrows raised.

Lacey gestured to the chair. "Of course."

"I know your daddy and I had our differences from time to time, but that was just business, never personal. I hope you know that."

God, this sounds like a scene from The Godfather, Lacey thought wryly. *Next, he'll make me an offer I can't refuse.* She didn't say anything, just nodded.

They made small talk for a couple minutes until they ran out of things to say, and an awkward silence enveloped them like a blanket. After a few more seconds, Copeland stood and shook the wrinkles out of his pressed jeans.

"It was great to see you, Lacey," he said. "If there's anything I can do…"

Lacey nodded and smiled. "Thank you, Mr. Copeland," she said. "I appreciate that."

"Anytime," Cowboy Carl said before he walked away. As he went, he greeted several other customers, working the room like an old-time politician, shaking hands and slapping backs. Lacey took a sip of her coffee and set the cup down, then sat staring out the window at the traffic on 26th Avenue South. Young people were standing in little knots on the sidewalk, talking, drinking coffee and soft drinks, smiling in the sunshine. She saw plenty of college shirts: Vanderbilt, Belmont, Tennessee State, Lipscomb; they were all well-represented. She thought of her college days in Knoxville, years before she would return to the city where she grew up for her father's funeral.

By the time she finished her coffee and stood up

to leave, the place was empty. Two young men were setting up a small stage at one end of the room for that evening's open mic night. On her way through the lobby, she noticed a signboard that read "Open Mic Tonite 7:00 Hosted by JT Wheeler". As she was walking by, a young man walked up to the sign and taped a paper over JT's name and wrote in the name of someone she didn't know.

Lacey's lawyer had an office on the 19th floor of the AT&T Building in downtown Nashville. Known to locals as "The Bat Building", it's the tallest building in the state, and the offices of O'Hurley & Grimm afforded her a stunning view of the river far below. But, she wasn't there to be wowed by the view. She was there to find out how to get that bitch Beverly thrown out of the house she shared with Big Jim and out of hers and her mother's lives forever.

"I'm sorry, Lacey," Neal Grimm told her. "As your father's wife, she's entitled to stay in the house. It was joint property. The business, however, is a different story. Your mother owns that outright."

"I know. She told me. But, Beverly doesn't deserve that house. I walked in the other day, and she was upstairs with one of the stable boys. My father's body wasn't even cold." Although she wanted to give the appearance of steely resolve, she was on the verge of tears. The lawyer noticed her welling up and slid a box of Kleenex across the desk to her.

"No matter what she was doing, or how much you dislike her, she owns the house now. Her sex life has no bearing," said Grimm, who had slept with Beverly himself on several occasions.

"This is crazy. My mother has to live in that little dollhouse, and Beverly gets the mansion in Belle Meade? How is that fair?"

"Fair or not, it's how your father set it up," Grimm replied. "I'm very sorry."

Lacey stood up. "Do you have a waste basket?" she asked, holding a handful of tissues.

"Of course," Grimm said, pushing his chair back from the desk. Before he could get up, Lacey went around the desk. He almost fell trying to intercept her. "I can take those," he said.

But he was too slow. Lacey came around to his side before he could block her path. On his blotter was a picture of Beverly Diamante that hadn't been visible from where she'd been sitting. In it she was wearing nothing but a pair of thong panties, her hands and arms strategically placed to hide her voluptuous breasts. Lacey stopped, her eyes flying open and her hand going to her mouth. Grimm quickly slid a folder over the photo.

"Don't jump to conclusions, Lacey," he said frantically. "Beverly is interested in modeling and I've agreed to represent her."

Lacey was beside herself. "You were my parents' lawyer for what, thirty years? How could you be involved with her? On any level?"

Grimm, who had sat back down, stood again and favored her with a condescending look. "I think we're done here. If there's nothing else?"

"No, nothing," Lacey murmured.

"Call me if you need anything," Grimm said. He shuffled some papers on his desk, waiting for her to leave.

"Sure," Lacey said, then added under her breath, "when Hell freezes over."

TWENTY-THREE

The day after JT was cleared of any involvement in Big Jim's murder by virtue of Mindy Barrish's assertion that they had been together, he was on another bus headed for Rhode Island. He had paid for his ticket himself, despite Kennedy's offer. He thought it was just the cop's way of ingratiating himself with him in an effort to get information. Besides, he had zero interest in speaking to either detective again.

As the bus backed out of its bay, JT leaned against the back of the seat with a tremendous feeling of relief. He stared absentmindedly out the window as they passed a series of industrial buildings; a couple of building supply companies, an auto body shop, and an enormous adult bookstore. The further the city he had come to love slipped behind him, the more relaxed he felt.

Two days later, he was back home and had finally begun to unwind. He hadn't brought his guitar with him, so he wasn't doing anything musical, just spending his time taking long walks trying to clear his head or sitting by the pool in his parents' backyard. After a couple days of this, he decided to take a walk to the gas station he was working at before he left for Nashville. When he got there, he discovered that all the guys he had been friendly with had moved on to other jobs. Anxious to find someone to have a beer with, he decided to go to the restaurant where he had met Sarah. When he went in, to his surprise, she was there.

Her eyes grew wide, her smile even wider. "JT!" she squealed, rushing to him, her arms wide open. "I can't believe it," she said, her words muffled by his chest. JT, completely shocked not only to see her but by her reaction, took a moment to return her hug. Once he did, though, he was reluctant to let go. Her hair smelled incredible. He didn't know what kind of shampoo she used, but he would have been happy to drown in it.

"I didn't know you were back here," he said, still hugging her.

"I've been back since May," she replied.

Finally, they let go of one another, and she took a step back from him. "Well, look at you, Mr. Successful Songwriter. How are you?"

JT shrugged. "I'm okay, I guess."

Sarah's eyes narrowed. "What's wrong?" she

asked.

"I'm just tired that's all," he lied.

"Uh huh," she said knowingly. "You'll tell me when you're ready, I guess."

"It's so great to see you," JT said, changing the subject. "Really great."

Suddenly, Sarah took his hand and started to lead him toward a table. "Come on," she said. "It's almost time for my break. Let's have something to eat, and you can stop fibbing to me and tell me what's wrong." She stopped at a booth in the front window of the restaurant and gave him a friendly shove. "Sit down," she ordered.

"No, Sarah, I'm not hungry."

"Sit," she repeated and placed a hand on his shoulder.

He obeyed this time. "Fine, maybe a Coke." Sarah hurried away and rushed back with two glasses as if she expected JT to try and escape while she was gone. She placed a glass and a paper-wrapped straw in front of him and slid into the other side of the booth, then surprised him by reaching across the table and squeezing his hand, then leaving hers covering it.

"I can't believe you're here. Are you okay, JT?" she asked, peering at him closely.

"Yeah," he shrugged, then added, "There's been some stuff going on, but I'm good."

"Ah," she said, nodding emphatically. "'Some stuff', huh? Now we're getting to it. What *kind* of stuff? A girl?"

JT, who had been staring out the window, looked back at her sharply, then grinned crookedly. "What? Aw, no, nothing like that." He shook his head as if to reinforce what he was saying.

"Are you seeing someone?" she asked, surprising him yet again, a twinkle in her pretty eyes. "Some southern belle, perhaps?" Her voice had taken on a sing-song, teasing quality that JT found very appealing. This was the last place he would have expected –or wanted, for that matter- the conversation to go, but he smiled and laughed in spite of himself.

"It's got nothing to do with a girl," he said, although he couldn't help but think, *What difference does that make to you? You're the one who's engaged. Or married, by now.* As he was thinking this, he glanced at her left hand, which was bare. *She just takes it off at work, so it doesn't get wrecked*, he told himself before he could start thinking maybe things had changed.

"Well, you obviously have some sort of problem. And what kind of problem do guys have beside us women?" she asked, laughing. "Either it's a girl or you murdered someone."

Nothing could have prepared her for JT's reaction. He had just lifted his glass to his mouth and was taking a drink. Suddenly, he put it on the table so hard that it broke, causing soda to flow across the table and into her lap. He sat staring at her, mouth agape. She jumped up, shocked, and grabbed at the napkin holder on the table.

JT started coughing as his mouthful of soda went down the wrong pipe. His face instantly turned bright red, then almost purple, and he stood. Sarah ran to his side and started pounding him on the back, her wet lap forgotten for the moment.

"Are you okay?" she asked him several times,

getting increasingly nervous as he tried, but couldn't, stop coughing. When he finally got himself under control, he slumped back into his seat, then jumped back up when he realized the soda had flown in his direction as well as hers.

"I'm sorry," he croaked, but she waved off the apology.

Her eyes were still wide. "JT? What happened?" But, before he could answer, two large parties came in, and she had to go back to work.

Before she walked away, she pointed at him. "Don't leave."

TWENTY-FOUR

Kennedy and Gray had just finished going over their suspect list again when Gray's phone rang. He answered it without looking to see who was calling.

"Gray." He looked at Kennedy, his eyes widening a bit; eyebrows arched. "Yes, sir. I understand. I will." He thumbed off the phone. "Chief again. He's getting some real pressure to release the body for the funeral. Seems Mrs. Diamante Number Two is in his office and just can't wait to put her husband in the ground. He's calling Bo to have Big Jim released."

"Man, that is one cold-blooded woman," Kennedy observed. "She's a snake. You think she'd be more concerned with finding out who killed him than how quickly she can plant him."

"Obviously, she wants this glossed over. So, if she doesn't want us to find the shooter, what does that tell you?"

"It tells me we're going to Belle Meade," Kennedy replied, rolling his eyes. "Or should we just go upstairs?"

"Why don't we head out to Belle Meade while she's here?" Gray suggested. "And if she doesn't get back while we're there, we'll wait for her and make sure she sees us, see what she does."

"Let the mind games begin!" Kennedy laughed. He stood up and took his sports coat off the back of his chair.

"Why don't you leave the jacket?" Gray asked. "For crying out loud, it's about a hundred degrees out there." Kennedy looked at him for a moment, debating with himself, then slipped it on.

"First, I'll stop wearing the jacket; then I'll show up in a polo shirt. Not long after that, I'll be working cases in bib overalls and a straw hat, barefoot, with a piece of grass hanging out of my mouth. Where will it end?"

Gray tried to respond, but he was laughing too hard.

The detectives were standing at the door of the late Big Jim Diamond's mansion once again. The ornate front door swung open, revealing a small, wiry black man in formal attire.

"May I help you?" he asked politely, his accent more reminiscent of New Orleans than Nashville. Gray introduced himself and Kennedy. "I'm afraid Mrs.

Diamante isn't at home," the man said. "Would you care to leave your card?"

"Actually," Gray said, "we'd like to talk to some of the employees. Why don't we start with you? You are?"

"Phillip Butler," the man replied. "And, yes, I'm aware of the irony." He smiled brightly. The detectives had no doubt he had gotten a lot of mileage out of that little *bon mot* over the years.

"And what do you do here, Mr. Butler?"

"Now, not much," Phillip replied. Although he maintained an air of detachment, it was clear to the detectives that he was aggravated about something.

"Now?" Gray asked. "Would that be since Big Jim's murder? Do you not get along with Mrs. Diamante?"

"Please, sir, I don't want to speak out of turn," Phillip said.

"We're all friends here, Phillip," Gray said, causing Phillip's smile to reappear. It was like watching the sun come out from behind the clouds. "I'm getting a vibe from you, and that vibe says you worked for Big Jim and tolerated his second wife. Am I in the ballpark?"

Phillip pressed his lips together. "You might say that," he allowed.

"May we come in?" Gray asked. Phillip immediately stepped aside so they could enter the house.

After they had talked for about fifteen minutes, with Phillip becoming increasingly more relaxed and happy to dish the dirt on Beverly by the second, the house phone rang.

Phillip excused himself and crossed the room, his heels clicking on the marble floor. "Diamante residence," he answered. He listened for a moment, then said, "Yes, ma'am" and hung up. The detectives were watching him.

"Her Majesty wants me to run a bath for her. She's had 'a trying day' and is 'utterly exhausted'. She demanded I do it personally. Her way of reminding me who's in charge now. Mr. Diamante treated me like a trusted friend; to her, I'm just an object, something she owns." A young woman happened through the room just then, dressed in a maid's uniform.

"Carla," Phillip said, "would you please run a hot bath for the Empress?" The girl smiled and nodded, then went up the stairs. Apparently, nobody on the staff held the lady of the house in any esteem. Phillip turned back to the detectives. "Mr. Diamante was a wonderful employer. He treated everyone who worked here with respect. He didn't demand, he asked. He didn't rant and fire people left and right like his widow. And he certainly didn't have relations with the staff. Or, if he did, he was so discreet no one ever knew. I don't think he did, though. Domestics tend to be quite chatty about such matters."

"So Beverly is sleeping with one of the workers here? Who is it?"

"It would be a much shorter list if I told you who it wasn't," Phillip said, shaking his head. "The woman is disgusting."

Gray reached out his hand to Phillip, who looked a little surprised, but then shook heartily.

"Thank you, Mr. Butler, we appreciate your help." Kennedy shook with him, too.

"Gentlemen," he said, nodding formally. "You're more than welcome. Likewise, I appreciate your treating me with respect and dignity. It doesn't happen much around here anymore."

As they walked out to their car, Gray turned back. "She was coming straight home?"

Phillip nodded but looked puzzled. "Yes."

"We're just going to sit in our car for a few minutes. Timing is everything." He winked and Phillip smiled broadly.

"Yes, sir!" he said, then shut the door behind them.

Kennedy started the engine so he could run the air conditioner, but waited until they saw a yellow car approaching from the direction of downtown to move. As it got closer, they could tell it was a vintage Corvette.

"Nice wheels," Kennedy said with a soft whistle.

When it got close enough, he put the car in gear and moved slowly down the driveway. Just as Beverly started to slow to turn in, he pulled out onto the road, making sure she got a good look at them.

"Did you see the look on her face?" Kennedy asked.

"Priceless," Gray said. "Let's head back."

Kennedy turned to look at him. "Five bucks says the chief calls you before we get to the station."

Gray shook his head and smiled. "I'm not betting against that, because I know that's exactly what's going to happen."

TWENTY-FIVE

The restaurant closed at nine. Despite the fact that his pants were wet, JT had stayed until closing. While he was waiting for Sarah to get off, he had used a roll of paper towels to mop up his mess despite Sarah's objections. After that, he sat looking out the window trying to decide if he should tell her his story. He finally decided he would, then spent the rest of the time wondering just how to do that without making himself sound like a jerk.

At ten past nine, Sarah came out of the back and they left. Once outside, they walked towards where she had parked her car. She leaned against the fender; her arms folded in front of her with a sweatshirt draped over them, so JT couldn't see that she still wasn't wearing a ring. She looked very anxious, and he wanted to pull her into his arms and comfort her, but he knew he shouldn't go there. True, he had made a habit of bedding already-attached women since he got to Nashville, but this was different. This was Sarah.

JT was reluctant to tell her the whole story, but once he started, it all came pouring out in a rush. Despite the sudden flood of words, he still managed to edit the details about where he was and what he was doing instead of writing with Chuck Kinsella, before he found Big Jim's body.

"You worked for Big Jim Diamond?" she asked, her voice full of wonder. "I saw all this on the news. I thought they said they didn't have any suspects, but you were one? How come?"

"Because they think Jim called me in so he could fire me for missing that writing session," he explained.

"That's crazy," she said. "Why would he fire you for missing one appointment?" Her eyes were flashing with anger. Sweet Sarah; always a fiercely loyal friend. JT shrugged, feeling guilty about not telling her how many appointments he had blown off to party. It occurred to him that she didn't know him anymore, and he was reluctant to reveal too much of who he'd become.

When he had finished talking, Sarah wrapped her arms around him and stroked the back of his head.

"I'm so sorry, JT. You didn't deserve all this." *If you only knew*, he thought. He wanted desperately to change the subject, but he couldn't think of anything to say. They were standing there in the dark parking lot holding each other, and his thoughts inexplicably turned to her fiancé.

"How's Ed?" he asked, and immediately regretted it. But, foolish as they were, the words were out there, seemingly hanging in the air between them, and there was no way to reel them back in.

"We broke up," Sarah said simply. JT let that swirl around his brain for a moment, and then, although it seemed surreal and incredibly poorly-timed given what he had just told her, he put a finger under her chin and tipped her face up to his. His whole body seemed to have become electrified, and he leaned toward her, tilting his head slightly. He had wanted this for so long. Just as their lips were about to touch, his phone rang in his pocket, and they both jumped.

He seemed to deflate right before her eyes, but she laughed and said, "You better answer it."

He swiped his finger –the same finger he had just touched her face with- across the screen and placed the phone up to his ear.

"Hi, Mom," he said with a wry smile, but the smile slipped from his face, and his eyes widened. "What?" he asked. "When? Oh, my God. Yeah, I'll be right home." He looked at Sarah. "I gotta go."

"I'll drive you," she said immediately, but JT shook his head vehemently.

"No, you don't want to get any closer to this than you have to," he said.

"You need to get home right away, so you're going to walk?" she asked. "Don't be ridiculous. Get in." Once in the car, she immediately took his hand. She wasn't surprised that it was sweaty. "Is someone sick?" she asked. "Or?" She didn't want to say the word.

JT looked at her. "No," he said, shaking his head, "nothing like that. The cops are at my house looking for me."

Sarah drove the few miles between the restaurant and JT's parents' house quickly, not quite observing the speed limit signs that dotted the road. As soon as they turned onto his street, they saw three cars —one marked and two not- parked in front of the house. JT felt his heart drop and glanced at Sarah, who was staring at the cars, her face pale in the dashboard lights.

"Oh, God," she whispered. "What's happening?"

"You should drop me off here," JT said, but Sarah shook her head.

"I'm coming with you. I waited too long to be with you. I'm sticking close."

JT turned to her, shocked by what she had just said. For a brief moment, he almost forgot about the police waiting for him fifty yards further up the street.

"What do you mean, 'waited too long'? When did you ever say you'd go out with me?"

Sarah took his hand. "When did you ever ask?" she replied gently, then drove toward the house.

TWENTY-SIX

Chief Wall had been in Captain Paulson's office earlier that afternoon, breathing fire about the Big Jim case, not coincidentally just after he received an irate call from the widow Diamante.

"I told the ME to release the body. Your guys have a cause of death, and they know who the killer is. What the hell is the hold-up?"

Paulson knew enough to tread lightly. "The suspect we had wasn't our guy," he said.

"I say he was," Wall countered.

"With all due respect, Chief, he has a solid alibi."

Wall snorted. "His alibi is Mindy Barrish. Do you know who she is? A bimbo who's chief claim to fame is she married some music big shot. I wouldn't take her word if she said the sky was blue. She's lying."

"Why?" Paulson asked. "Why would she lie? What does she get out of it?"

"She gets her name in the papers for a day or two, her fifteen minutes. It's him, Wheeler. Bring him in. And keep him this time. And tell them to stay the hell away from Bev Diamante!" He turned and stormed out of the office. All of the detectives in the room quickly turned back to their desks and tried to look as if they hadn't been listening.

As soon as Sarah stopped in front of the house, two uniformed policemen approached the car. JT saw with dismay that he knew one of them, and his stomach did a slow-motion flip. In fact, they had known each other since elementary school, had been in Cub Scouts and played Little League together. Just when he thought it couldn't get worse, it did. Now everyone he knew growing up would know all about this. JT opened the car door and stepped out.

"Hi, Pete," he said, completely unsure how to interact with his sometime friend and occasional nemesis.

"JT," Pete said curtly with a quick nod.

"How you doing?" JT ventured, but Pete shook his head.

"This isn't a social call, JT. I have to take you in."

"For what?" JT asked, genuinely confused. Sarah was watching this whole exchange with a horrified look on her face. She recognized Pete. She didn't really know him but had seen him in the restaurant on numerous occasions. She had even waited on him a handful of times. He had always seemed like an immature jerk to her, the kind of guy who had been a bully growing up and loved the power he felt being a cop.

"Why are you doing this?" she asked him.

Pete turned to her. "Ma'am, you'd be well-advised to stay out of this. In fact, I'm going to suggest you clear the area." He nodded at the other uniformed officer, who immediately stepped up to Sarah and began to maneuver her back around to the driver's side of her car.

"JT!" she wailed.

"Go, Sarah," he said, although he wished she could stay with him. "I'll call you as soon as I can."

"Let go of me," Sarah said suddenly.

Then JT heard his father's voice. "Take your hands off her!" The elder Wheeler rushed past where his son was standing, in the direction that the cop had moved Sarah.

"Just put me in the car before this gets any worse," JT pleaded. Pete opened the door for him. As soon as he slid in, the detective, who until now hadn't said a word, leaned in the open passenger window as Pete got into the front.

"Nashville PD wants us to hold you until they can get someone here to bring you back with them."

"But, they cleared me," JT insisted, incredulous. "I have an alibi. They released me."

"I guess they changed their minds," the detective said, then moved away.

"Look, JT," Pete said in a low voice from the driver's seat, "We're just doing our jobs. Don't make it harder than it has to be."

JT's mother had been watching this unfold from the front door, but now she had come outside. As she approached the police car, she burst into tears, which set his father off.

"What the hell do you people think you're doing?" he yelled. "You grab my son, who was cleared of the false charges against him, you manhandle a young lady, you upset my wife... Are we in Nazi Germany?" JT leaned his head back against the seat and closed his eyes, wishing for an end to this nightmare. He opened them just in time to see the splash from the headlights as Sarah drove past.

The detective had gone over to where JT's parents were huddled together and was speaking to them quietly. He even had a companionable arm over Mr. Wheeler's shoulder. Finally, it seemed like things were under control. JT looked out the back windshield of the cruiser and spotted Sarah's car down the street, lights off. Apparently, she'd driven around the block and was parked a few houses away, watching. Now he looked at the house across the street and saw the curtains in the picture window twitch.

"Bastards, JT thought. Are you enjoying the show, you miserable pricks? And, bad as this was for him, he could only imagine the turmoil his parents were experiencing. He didn't even want to think about that.

TWENTY-SEVEN

Buddy Carlisle was sitting on his backyard patio when his wife opened the sliding door that led into their kitchen.

"Buddy, there are detectives her to see you." She looked curious, but not overly concerned. After all, she never thought for a minute that her husband of twenty-five years had anything to do with Big Jim's murder.

"Should I show them to the living room or do you want them to come out?" she asked.

Buddy studied her face. He could see how hard this whole thing had been on her, almost as hard as it had been on him. She had known and been friends with Jim for years.

"I'll see them out here," he said, the weight of this whole ordeal pressing down on him like an anvil. "Thanks, sweetheart." His wife, Barbara, flashed him a smile and disappeared into the house. Gray and Kennedy were still standing on the front stoop when Barbara got to the door.

"I'm sorry. You didn't have to wait out there, gentlemen," she said, pulling the door all the way open. "Please come in. Buddy's out back." She led them through the house and outside.

Gray was surprised by how much Buddy seemed to have aged since they had met the day of the murder. He could swear there was more gray in his hair, and he looked like he had lost weight. His complexion was sallow.

"Thank you, Mrs. Carlisle," Gray said, smiling. She disappeared back into the house.

"We thought you'd like to know," Gray said to Buddy, "that we talked to JT Wheeler. He had an alibi.

"Thank God," Buddy said, relief washing across his face. "I knew he couldn't have done this."

"He ran," Gray said. "It's been my experience that innocent people don't do that but, in this case, my experience didn't hold up." Buddy stared off into the distance, then swiped at his eyes, which had taken on a shine.

"Either of you want a beer?" he said. Gray glanced at several empty bottles lined up on the picnic table. It didn't escape Buddy. "They're not all mine," he said. "My brother and his son stopped by to see how I was doing."

Gray nodded. "Not our business anyway, Mr. Carlisle," he said. "But, while we're here, we'd like to ask you about a few people whose names came up during the investigation.

"Of course," Buddy said. "I'll help any way I can."

"We appreciate that," Kennedy said, opening his ever-present notebook.

"I know there were people who didn't like Big Jim, but a lot of that was just jealousy. A lot of guys who were in at the beginning couldn't handle the changes that came along, but Jim was like a chameleon; he could adapt to anything."

"How so?" Gray asked.

"Jim worked with Eddy Arnold, who was a huge star in the forties and fifties, and he worked with Ari Fox, who's one of the biggest stars around these days. He changed as the business changed and was successful every time. But, he didn't just react; he also orchestrated a lot of those changes. He completely transcended Country music.

"Can you think of anyone specifically who might have had enough of a problem with him to want him dead?"

Buddy shook his head. "No, no one." He sniffed and blinked back tears. "I still can't believe this. Jim was like a father to me. And JT was like my little brother," he added.

"I know," Kennedy soothed, "and I'm sorry for your loss."

"Thank you," Buddy said, rubbing his red, raw eyes.

"So, names that have come up...Cowboy Carl?"

Buddy made a face like he smelled something awful. "Copeland's a jackass, pardon my language.

Nobody likes him because he's always complaining about some slight or other, real or imagined."

"Apparently, he was on the phone with Big Jim when he was killed."

"So wouldn't that clear him right off?" Buddy asked.

"It depends on where he was calling from," Gray answered. "He was on his cell phone."

"I doubt it was him anyway," Buddy said, shaking his head.

"Oh? Why do you say that?"

"He just never struck me as the type. He's more of an 'all talk' kind of guy. Even in negotiations, he'd talk tough and then fold almost immediately. He's a big mouth, but that's about it."

"What about Dixie Lee Wrenn?"

Buddy did a double take. "Dixie Lee?" His eyes narrowed. "Why are you asking about her?"

"Her name came up in our investigation," Kennedy said, watching him for a reaction. "Are you surprised?"

Buddy sighed. "Jim and Dixie had a complicated relationship. There always seemed to be some bad blood between them. Her mother, too. Polly June. I don't know what went on between those three, but, even saying that, Dixie's a sweet girl. She couldn't possibly be involved."

"What about his wives? What's your take on them?" Gray asked. No sooner had he spoken then his phone rang. "Excuse me," he said to Buddy, then took a few steps away. "Gray. What? When? Jesus Christ!" He put the phone back in his pocket and looked at Kennedy. "We have to go." He gestured toward the side yard. "Can we got this way?" Buddy nodded and the detectives rushed around to the front of the house, Buddy trailing behind.

"What now?" Kennedy asked as they took off down the street.

"JT Wheeler is being held in Rhode Island awaiting extradition," he said grimly.

Barbara Carlisle was standing at the front door, looking out at her husband, who was staring down the street.

"Is everything okay?" she called to him. He turned to her with a perplexed look on his face.

"I don't know. They asked about Margie and Beverly, then one of them got a call and they went racing off. It was strange."

"Why don't you come in?" she smiled. "I just made some iced tea."

Buddy took a last look in the direction the detectives had gone, then crossed the lawn to the front door.

TWENTY-EIGHT

While they were waiting for JT to be brought back from Rhode Island, the detectives were discussing what their next move should be.

"What say we take a run at this Dixie character?" Gray offered. "Sounds like she had as much of a motive as anyone."

Kennedy glanced up from the notes on his desk. Gray didn't know how he kept track of where he wrote what; his desktop was covered with paper. Over the five years they'd been partnered-up, he had learned that the younger detective had a ridiculous ability to keep it all in order, and for that he was grateful. He, Gray, had never been a note-taker; it was always his partners, beginning with Lonnie Bergen, who had taken on that role.

Kennedy stood up and slipped into his jacket and they left.

"Dixie, where's my gun?" Rusty Sills was standing next to the couch, rubbing the stubble on his jawline, scared of what she might tell him.

Dixie turned to look at him. "I don't know," she replied, crying softly.

Rusty grabbed her by the shoulders and gave her a gentle shake. "Where is it?" he demanded, but she just shook her head and cried harder. Rusty was beside himself. He knew Dixie had hated Big Jim, although he could never get her to tell him why. But, he'd heard rumors –vile, disgusting rumors- and now he'd discovered his pistol wasn't in the bedside table drawer where he kept it. Word was Jim had been shot with a twenty-two, the same caliber as Rusty's missing piece. He started pacing again.

"Jesus," he muttered, rubbing hard at his forehead. What had Dixie said to him about Jim when she'd come to collect him at the bar the other day? Something about helping himself, he thought. What was it? What did that mean, 'helping himself'? To a song? To *her?* He didn't want to believe that, couldn't believe that. It couldn't be true, could it? If so, it would turn everything he'd ever known about Big Jim Diamond on its head. Rusty willed himself to focus, but the memory kept turning up at the edge of his mind, tantalizingly out of reach, turning over and over, always slightly out of focus. He went back to where Dixie was curled up on the couch.

"Help me out here, Dix," he urged. "Where's the gun?" Her eyelids fluttered open, and she tried to sit up, but only made it halfway.

"I dunno, Rusty," she said. Rusty thought she seemed to be having trouble forming the words. "Shtop ashking me," she slurred, her voice trailing off.

Rusty shook her again. "Wake up, Dixie Lee. You mind me, now."

"Stop it, Rusty," she moaned and lay back down. "Leave me be." Rusty was leaning down toward her again when, from the corner of his eye, he noticed something under the rocking chair he favored. He walked toward it like a man in a dream; the closer he got, the clearer it became what it was. He picked up the empty pill bottle and turned it so he could read the label. Sleeping pills. All at once he realized what she had done and he rushed to the kitchen to dial nine-one-one. Less than five minutes later, Dixie was in an ambulance on her way to the hospital, a tearful Rusty squeezed in next to her, stroking her clammy hand.

When the detectives got to Dixie's apartment, there had been no answer. They had heard a radio call come in that someone at that address had been rushed to the hospital, but no name was given, so they drove back to the station. Just before he sat down at his desk, Kennedy happened to glance into the break room, where several officers were standing with their backs to him, staring at a television mounted high in a corner. Behind the news anchor, they were showing a picture of a pretty blonde woman along with the caption "Songbird Crashes". Kennedy walked quickly into the room just as the report ended and the station's weatherman appeared in front of a map of the area. He grabbed the arm of one of the detectives in the room.

"Hey," Kennedy said.

"Hey, Brett."

What was that all about?" he asked.

"Some country singer OD'd," the man replied.

"Dixie Lee Wrenn?"

The other detective appeared surprised. "You've heard of her?" he asked.

"Yeah, she's a person of interest in our case," Kennedy said. He trotted to where Gray had just sat down and picked up his phone. "Come on. I know where Dixie Lee is."

Gray replaced the receiver with a clatter and followed his partner.

Dixie Lee had had her stomach pumped and been dosed with charcoal to absorb whatever residue was still in her from the pills she swallowed. She heard an almost-whispered conversation going on around her, but kept her eyes closed while she tried to figure out what was going on. She didn't recognize the voices.

Suddenly, someone said, "She's faking."

"I assure you, Detective, she's not faking," a second voice responded. "I worked on her in the ER. She took half a bottle of pills."

"I'm sure she did, Doc, but I meant she's faking now. She's awake and listening to every word we're saying."

"Miss Wrenn?" This time, the voice came from right next to her head. She opened her eyes slowly, hoping to preserve her ruse and give the appearance that she was just now waking up. The man immediately next to her was obviously a doctor, but now a second face swam into focus.

"I don't have time for games," Gray said roughly. "I want to talk to you about Mr. Sills' gun. Did you take it?"

Dixie nodded slowly. She may have been technically awake, but she wasn't yet fully functioning.

"Did you go to Big Jim Diamond's office with it?" Another nod. "Did you shoot him, Miss Wrenn?" Dixie didn't answer right away, and the air in the room felt eerily still as they waited for her response. But, then Dixie shook her head emphatically, tossing her hair back and forth. "You took the gun with you to see Big Jim, but you're not the one who shot him? Is that your story?" Dixie Lee began to cry.

"Detective, please," the doctor interjected, but Gray paid him no attention. "I'm going to have to ask you to leave now. You're getting her too upset." Gray turned a stern gaze on him, and the man quickly cast his eyes at the floor, then turned to Kennedy. "Please go," he pleaded, then found a sliver of courage, "before I'm forced to call security."

"Fine," Gray said. He pulled out his handcuffs, took Dixie's left arm -the one without the IV- and cuffed her to the bed. "As soon as a uniformed officer gets here, we'll go."

The doctor gestured to the cuffs. "Is that really necessary?" he asked, clearly upset.

"Yes," Gray said, nodding. "Yes, it is."

The doctor assumed a superior tone. "Detective, I assure you Ms. Wrenn is in no condition to *make a break for it.*" He favored Gray with a patronizing smirk and he responded with a steely stare.

"Doctor, I don't tell you how to do your job, so don't try to tell me how to do mine." The doctor's shoulders slumped, and he turned and left the room.

Twenty minutes later, one of Nashville's Finest was seated just outside the door to Dixie Lee's hospital room. Rusty was inside with her and Dixie, who was fully awake now, was yelling at him.

"Pipe down in there," the officer said, leaning into the doorway.

"Sorry," Rusty replied, then lowered his voice. "Dixie, I had to."

"No, Rusty, you didn't have to," Dixie insisted in a loud whisper. "How could you do that to me? They think I murdered Jim." When he didn't respond, she said, "What? You think so, too? Get out, Rusty, and don't bother coming back."

"Dixie," Rusty pleaded, "I'm on your side."

"Yeah, going to the cops really proved that, now, didn't it? I can't believe this." She started crying.

"Dixie, you always had a problem with Big Jim. First you steal my gun, and he turns up dead, shot with the same caliber pistol. Then you try to kill yourself."

"I did *not*, Rusty! How could you even think that about me? God! I didn't shoot him, and I didn't try to kill myself. I just wanted to sleep."

"Yeah, permanently. You don't take half a bottle of pills just to sleep."

This back and forth went on for a few more minutes before Rusty gave up and walked out of the room.

"I'm sorry about that," he said to the cop when he passed him. "I'm going to the cafeteria for a coffee.

You want anything?" The cop shook his head, and Rusty made his way down the hallway to the bank of elevators, walking like a far older man than he was. He pushed the down button, then leaned against the wall, head hanging, utterly spent.

TWENTY-NINE

The morning after she took the sleeping pills, Dixie Lee was released from the hospital. She had spent two hours with the hospital shrink and been able to convince her that she didn't intentionally overdose and had no intention of harming herself. Although the doctor wanted to admit her for observation, she eventually relented with the caveat that Rusty wouldn't leave her alone. Dixie agreed, and Rusty called for a cab to take them home.

He was relieved that Dixie still wanted him around, but, as soon as they got downstairs and out to the sidewalk where the taxi was waiting, she set him straight.

"Don't you go thinking we're all right, Rusty Sills, 'cause we're not. I'll never forgive you for what you did, do you understand me?"

"But, Dix…"

"Don't you 'Dix' me," she hissed. Rusty reached for the car door, but Dixie pushed past him and slid into the back seat. "I'm going home. Alone."

Rusty put his hand on the door before she could close it and shook his head sadly. "You don't want to do that, Dixie Lee, 'cause if you do I'm gonna go right back inside and tell that to the doctor. She'll see to it that you get admitted."

Dixie Lee glared at him. "I guess I should have known you'd rat me out again, huh, Rusty?" Her blue eyes flashed with anger, and he finally looked away.

"Fine," he said, thoroughly defeated. "You do what you need to do, Dixie Lee. You know where to find me."

"Yeah, on a barstool at Sonny's, no doubt." She yanked the door shut, leaving Rusty standing forlornly on the sidewalk. All he could do was watch her go.

As this little drama was playing out, Kennedy called the hospital to get an update on Dixie's condition and was told she had been released. When he hung up, he conveyed the news to Gray, who immediately suggested they go talk to her. Her actions the previous night had pushed her up the suspect list. They pulled up in front of her apartment just as she was getting out of a Checker Cab. When she saw them, a deer-in-the-headlights look bloomed in her eyes. She looked tired, but otherwise fine, if a little pale.

"Miss Wrenn, we'd like to talk to you," Gray said

as they approached her.

Dixie Lee shook her head. "Why can't you just leave me alone?" she asked. "I don't have nothing to tell you."

"Oh, I think you do," Gray countered. "The only question is, would you rather do it here or down at the station?" They could almost hear the options Dixie Lee was clicking through in her head, but finally her shoulders sagged.

"Won't you come in, gentlemen?" she said, her voice dripping with sarcasm.

The apartment was set up so you entered into the living room, which is where Dixie was when she lost consciousness. Both detectives immediately saw the empty pill bottle on an end table. Dixie walked over and slipped it into the pocket of her jeans.

"Have a seat," she said, now resigned to the situation.

'Thank you," Kennedy said.

"You'll forgive me if I don't offer you tea and crumpets. I gave the maid the day off."

Gray ignored her sarcasm. "Where's your friend, Mr. Sills?" he asked.

Dixie snorted derisively. "I don't know where Judas is. Probably drowning his sorrows somewhere. How much booze will thirty pieces of silver buy these days?"

"You understand he saved your life, right?" Gray asked her. "You do know that?"

"What I know, Detective, is that if it weren't for him, you and I wouldn't be having this conversation. Now please just ask your questions so I can lie down.

I'm exhausted."

The detectives were back in the car, driving toward Marjorie Diamante's house.

"Some story, huh?" Kennedy commented. Dixie told them she had gone to confront Big Jim, not about a song she thought he stole from her, but because she had found out something about him the night before. It turned out that Big Jim Diamond, Grand Ol' Opry legend and her rapist, was also her father.

"I went there to kill him," she'd sobbed once the story started to come out. At times, she spoke so fast that Kennedy, although writing frantically, had a hard time keeping up. "He laughed at me. I started crying and waving the gun around. He came at me and grabbed the gun away and put it on the desk. Then he…" She'd started sobbing uncontrollably at this point. It took her a full five minutes to calm down and, when she did, her voice came out in a ragged whisper. "He tried to kiss me. I pushed him away and ran out of the office. Ask Margie."

"Margie Diamante?" Kennedy asked, and Dixie Lee nodded. "She was there, too?"

Gray tried to convince her to call Rusty to stay with her, but she wouldn't hear of it, so he finally called the squad and had one of the female detectives come to the apartment. By the time she arrived, Dixie was curled up on the couch in the fetal position, sound asleep.

When they arrived at Margie's and knocked on the front door, they got no response. They were about to leave when they heard a woman's voice.

"Margie, there's someone at your door." They looked to see a woman in the window of the house next door. "She's coming," she said. Gray waved his thanks just as Margie came around the corner from the side yard, carrying a basket full of roses and a pair of pruning shears.

"Hello, detectives," she said with a smile. "I was just cutting some flowers for the table in the entry."

THIRTY

Gray and Kennedy were sitting in Margie's living room again, corroborating Dixie's story. If it were true that she ran out of the office when Jim took the gun away from her, then she couldn't be the killer.

"I went to discuss some expenditures Jim had made that I didn't think the business, meaning me, should pay for. I don't know why, but the parking lot door was open. It was supposed to be locked at all times after business hours. I went in and heard Jim laughing. Then I heard a woman. She was crying hysterically. I've known Dixie Lee for twenty-five years, and I didn't even recognize her voice. She was accusing him of horrible, dreadful things, and he wasn't disputing a word she said."

"How long did you listen for?" Kennedy asked.

"Not long, probably not even a minute."

"And you never went into his office?"

"No, I was in a state of shock. The woman, well, now I know it was Dixie Lee, was saying he was her father, and he slept with her even though he knew. I thought I was going to be sick. Then Dixie came running out, and I just grabbed her and led her outside. I thought for sure Jim was going to follow her, and I wanted to get her out of there as quickly as I could. The phone rang as we were leaving. The last thing I heard was Jim talking to someone like he didn't have a care in the world, like that whole ugly, disgusting episode had never happened."

"Why didn't you tell us all this before?" Gray asked.

Margie sighed. "I should have. I'm sorry. But, I knew Jim was alive when Dixie came out of the office, so I wanted to spare her from any...I don't know...I just didn't want to involve her and have all this come out. My God, this is hard enough on her without having it become public knowledge. And I knew she hadn't done anything, so I never expected her to be a suspect."

"It must have been hard for you, too," Gray said sympathetically.

"That's an understatement," Margie told them. "I'm devastated. I still feel sick to my stomach whenever I think about it. I've been avoiding going to the office, even though I need to get in there. Everything's in limbo right now, but I have to do payroll and pay the bills. It's surreal to think that business just goes on."

"We can take you now if you want," Gray offered. "It might be easier than going alone."

Margie considered the offer for a moment, then nodded. "Yes, I think so. If you're sure it's no trouble. Thank you, Detective."

"No trouble at all," Gray said. "One more thing; what time did this occur?"

"Around five thirty-five, I would think."

"Are you sure?"

"Yes, I happened to look at the mantel clock on my way out of the house. It was five thirty, and it's a five or six-minute walk."

Margie stopped outside the door, her key in her hand. Gray reached past her and broke the crime scene seal, and she unlocked it so the three of them could go in. She went up the stairs but stopped on the landing outside Diamond in the Rough and looked back at Gray.

"How bad is it in there?" she asked, looking ashen in the dim light. She was wearing a black blouse, and her head seemed to float above her body in the gloom.

"It's pretty bad," Gray admitted, remembering the blood-splattered picture. "Are you sure you feel up to it?"

"I have to do it sooner or later," she said and unlocked the door. "Maybe I can just take what I need and sit at Penny's desk in the front office."

"We'll help you get everything as quickly as possible," Kennedy assured her. They followed her in.

The first thing any of them noticed was that the office felt unused and stuffy, with the faint coppery scent of blood mixed with a note of sulfur. It was obvious it was a nice, airy space under normal conditions, but now it felt extremely claustrophobic and gloomy. Several plants were withered and dusty. The detectives purposely left the lights off so Margie wouldn't have to see every detail under the glare of the fluorescent strips in the ceiling -which Jim had seldom used- or the soft spotlights that made the pictures and awards stand out.

Once she was in Big Jim's office, Margie began quickly gathering up invoices and other items she needed. She handed everything to Kennedy, who took it out into the outer office for her. She avoided looking at the bloody areas as much as she could. Suddenly, she stopped and stared at the desk, seemingly taking a mental inventory.

Gray noticed her and asked, "Are you okay?"

"Where's the spindle?" she asked, then looked around the office.

"Ma'am?" Gray said

"There was a spindle on the desk. Penny used to put Jim's phone messages on it."

"Maybe he put it somewhere else or threw it out."

"He would never have thrown it out," Margie protested. "I gave it to him the same year he started the business because he was always complaining that his phone messages got lost before he could return calls. He went on about it so much that I went to an office supply store and looked for one for him. Finally, I found one in an antique shop. It was the biggest one I'd ever seen. I told Jim it was because he was going to be so successful that he needed one that would hold a lot of messages. It was a running joke with us. When he moved in here, he took it with him and his secretaries always knew to put his messages on it. Where could it be?" Gray took her by the arm and gently steered her out of Jim's office.

"I guess I'll need to call someone to clean up," she sniffed.

"Don't worry about that right now. Maybe Mr. Carlisle can help with whatever arrangements you need to make."

Margie nodded, then said, "But, where could the spindle be?" She was dabbing at her eyes with a tissue and her voice had an odd, disjointed quality to it like she was in shock. "I know how silly this must seem to you under the circumstances, me worrying about something like that.

"No, it doesn't sound silly at all," Gray said gently, which brought a small smile to her face.

"I'll find it," Gray assured her. But, he didn't. He looked through the built-in cabinets, the desk drawers, under the desk, and in the coat closet, but it was nowhere to be found.

THIRTY-ONE

"Detective?" Gray looked up from his desk. A uniformed officer was standing in the doorway. "Someone to see you. She asked for the detective who was working the Big Jim case."

"Did you get a name?"

"No," the officer replied, smiling lewdly, "but she's smoking hot. I sure wouldn't mind, if you catch my drift." He held out his hand and made a back and forth gesture.

Gray stood up and gave him a dirty look. "Thanks," he said, "that's real helpful. Try not to scrape your knuckles on the floor on the way back to your cave." It's not that Gray didn't appreciate a beautiful woman, but he hated when other men objectified them. It was one of his pet peeves. He made an effort to treat everyone with respect, even suspects, not that *that* was always possible. Still, he tried. He walked out of the office and headed for the visitors' area.

The officer turned to Kennedy. "What's his problem?" he asked.

"He's a strange guy," Kennedy replied. "He actually thinks women are people if you can believe that. You probably don't want to be here when he gets back."

"Yeah, yeah. You guys get your gold shields, and you forget where you came from," the man groused. "Maybe he switched teams after his wife dumped him."

Kennedy stood up. "Go, Peyton," he said, "before I help you along." The officer, Jed Peyton, was about to respond, but then he took a good look at Kennedy's expression and left without another word. Thirty seconds later, Gray came in with a young woman in tow. Peyton might have been a jerk about it, but he was right; she was a looker. About five-seven with long, light brown hair and striking green eyes set in a beautiful face, she attracted considerable attention from the men in the room.

"Have a seat, Miss Diamante," he said, catching Kennedy's eye. "This is my partner, Detective Kennedy. You have our deepest sympathies."

"Thank you," Lacey murmured. She was dressed all in black, apparently having come straight from the funeral. Big Jim Diamond had been laid to rest that morning, at his wife's insistence.

Can I get you anything? Coffee? Water?"

"No, thank you," Lacey said, folding her hands on

her lap and getting right down to business. "I know who killed my father. Or, who had him killed."

Gray leaned forward. "Really? Who?"

"His wife, Beverly." She all but spat the name out, as if it were something that tasted horrible.

"So, you think you know, or you know?" Gray asked.

Lacey sagged a bit in her chair and sighed. "I mean, I'm pretty sure..."

"Okay, why don't you take a deep breath and tell me why you think she had something to do with it." Lacey started with the pre-nuptial agreement, the alleged affairs, up to the day she went to the house and found that Beverly was upstairs with one of the farmhands.

"Well, it's clear you have a problem with your stepmother..."

"She is *not* my stepmother," Lacey said angrily. "She's a gold digging whore who manipulated my father into leaving my mother for her." The detectives were shocked, both by her vitriol and the word 'whore' coming out of that sweet face.

"I apologize," Gray said. "But, being a lousy wife doesn't translate to being a murderer."

"Oh, and she's been sleeping with my father's lawyer."

"How do you know that?" Kennedy asked.

"I saw a half-naked picture of her on his desk. He gave me some lame excuse about helping her with her modeling career, but he didn't want me to see it. But, it wasn't just what she was wearing; it was the way she was posing, like she was auditioning for a dirty movie."

"Again, her cheating doesn't make her a murderer.

Do you have any other evidence? Anything at all?"

"No," Lacey sighed, then stood up. "I'm sorry to have wasted your time."

"Hold on," Gray said, then he stood up, too. "I didn't say we weren't going to look into it. What's the lawyer's name?"

Twenty minutes later, the detectives stepped off the elevator onto the 19th floor of the AT&T building, where the offices of O'Hurley and Grimm took up the whole floor.. When they approached the receptionist, she told them that Mr. Grimm was with a client and couldn't be disturbed.

"That's okay," Gray said with a pleasant smile. "We'll wait." He sat down and started to thumb through a magazine.

"I'm afraid he's going to be tied up all afternoon," the woman told him, obviously hoping they'd leave.

"That's perfectly fine," Gray said, still smiling. "I'm a very patient man." He looked back down at his magazine. Kennedy was flipping through that day's USA Today. Suddenly the door behind the reception desk swung open, and a woman walked out, followed by a small, slim man who looked more like a mortician that a lawyer. They both appeared slightly disheveled.

Gray stood up. "Mr. Grimm?" he asked. The man retreated hurriedly into his office and shut the door. They heard the 'snick' of the door being locked.

The receptionist looked panicked. "I told you; Mr. Grimm is not available."

Gray turned on her. "Well, it looks to me like Mr. Grimm just became available. And if you don't want to face an obstruction charge, you'll be quiet and stay out of this."

"How dare you?" the woman sputtered. The client who had just come out of the office had stopped near the elevator and was watching them. Gray gave her a stern look, and she immediately turned away and started slapping at the down button.

Gray looked at Kennedy, then took out his handcuffs. "Let me have your hands," he said to the terrified woman. She certainly hadn't signed up for this.

She leaned heavily on the intercom button. "Mr. Grimm," she wailed. The door opened again.

"Just what is going on here?" Grimm demanded, pulling himself up to his full five-foot-six.

Gray flashed his badge. "We'd like to speak to you about the Diamantes, but your receptionist isn't being very accommodating." He was swinging the handcuffs back and forth on his index finger.

Grimm looked back and forth between the woman and Gray, then sagged. "Very well," he said, "but I can only spare a minute." The two detectives followed him into the office. "Have a seat," he said, although he remained standing.. As soon as they had, Grimm looked at them with a smug smile and said, "I'm afraid anything having to do with Mr. or Mrs. Diamante is protected by attorney-client privilege, as I'm sure you know." He sat down. "Sorry I couldn't be of more help," he smirked. "Shut the door on your way out, won't you?"

Gray smiled but didn't budge. "That client who just left…"

"Again, privileged."

"Why was her lipstick messed up? And her hair,

too?" Grimm's smile turned into a scowl. "Just what kind of a meeting was that, anyway?" Gray asked.

"That's none of your business," Grimm sniveled. Gray reached forward and plucked a picture frame off the desk and studied the snapshot in it.

"Put that down," the lawyer demanded.

"And your meetings with Beverly Diamante, were those the same kind of meetings as the one you just had?" Grimm sucked in his lips until his mouth was nothing more than a thin slit. "Nice looking family you have here," Gray said. He turned the picture so Kennedy could see it. "Isn't that a nice-looking family, Brett?"

"Nice," Kennedy agreed.

Gray looked back at the lawyer. "I'll bet you'd get your clock cleaned in a divorce, huh?" He was speaking in a friendly, conversational tone that was in stark contrast to the obvious threat he was making. He put the picture back on the desk. "So, what's it going to be, Mr. Grimm? Are you going to talk to us or do we need to pay a visit to your pretty wife?"

"Get out!" Grimm demanded, pointing at the door. He pulled a business card out of his top desk drawer and held it out. "If you want to speak to me again, call my attorney first." Gray noticed his hand was shaking quite badly, which pleased him.

THIRTY-TWO

First thing the next morning, the detectives drove back to the AT&T building and made themselves comfortable in the waiting area of O'Hurley and Grimm, much to the dismay of the receptionist. After a couple of nervous minutes, she picked up the phone and pushed an extension.

"Mr. Grimm, those detectives are here again. Yes, sir." She replaced the handset and looked up at Gray. "I'm sorry; Mr. Grimm is unavailable today. He said he'd be happy to meet with you tomorrow."

Gray smiled. "Well, now, that will be fine. Tell Mr. Grimm that, if he's not at the station at nine o'clock sharp tomorrow morning, I'll have the district attorney swear out an arrest warrant for him, and I'll serve it personally. Got it?" The receptionist nodded. "Good. You have a nice day."

In the elevator, Kennedy asked, "You think he'll show up?"

"Yep," Gray replied. "Him and his lawyer."

Gray and Kennedy were waiting in an interview room when Neal Grimm came in the following day. As Gray had predicted, he was accompanied by an attorney, an obese and quite tall, shaggy-haired man with a bushy beard and a nose full of broken blood vessels. To Gray, he looked like the type of man whose complexion would always be florid and would constantly seem as if he were trying to catch his breath.

"Jeffrey Leary, representing Mr. Grimm," the attorney informed them in a tone that was meant to let them know he didn't suffer fools gladly and that his time was infinitely more valuable than theirs. He placed his briefcase on the table with a loud 'thump'.

Gray smiled. "Wow, that's a heavy case," he remarked. "You must be a good lawyer."

Leary peered over his glasses briefly, but otherwise ignored the snipe. "Shall we get down to business? Mr. Grimm and I are quite busy."

"Well," Gray said, "We're certainly sorry that you gentlemen had to take time out of your busy schedule because we just usually sit around playing backgammon." Leary sneered. "We'll make this as quick as possible," Gray added. He flipped open a folder and pulled out a list of questions. "What is your relationship with Beverly Diamante?"

"Mrs. Diamante is a client," Leary answered.

Gray shot him a look, then turned back to Grimm.

"Do you have a personal relationship with her as well?"

"I already told you, she's a client," Leary said.

Gray looked at him, then back at Grimm. "Are you a ventriloquist, Mr. Grimm? If not, why don't you answer my questions instead of him."

"I've advised Mr. Grimm to let me handle this," Leary said.

"Fine," Gray said. "Play games with us. That'll do you a lot of good at trial."

"Trial?" Grimm exploded, almost shooting up out of his chair. "What are you talking about?"

Leary put a hand on his arm. "Let me handle this, Neal."

"No," Grimm said, shaking his head. "I'll answer their damn questions."

"Neal, I don't think that's a good idea," Leary warned.

"You're not the one they're talking about taking to trial," Grimm shot back.

Leary shot him a patronizing look. "They're bluffing, Neal."

Gray ignored Leary and focused his attention on Neal Grimm. "Well, good," Gray said in his most soothing voice. "I have your attention, do I?"

"Ask your questions," Grimm said, which made Leary shake his head.

"I can't advise you strongly enough, Neal..."

Gray fixed him with a hard look. "Your client wants to talk to us, so why don't you stand down?" Leary huffed. "So, Mr. Grimm, do you have a personal relationship with Mrs. Diamante?"

"No, strictly attorney, client."

"So, the naked picture you have of her is for what purpose?"

Grimm blanched, clearly caught off guard, then quickly collected himself. "I'm representing her in a new career venture," Grimm replied, barely missing a beat. "Modeling." Gray noticed he glanced away when he answered.

"Are you sure? She seems a little long in the tooth to be just starting out as a model." Grimm swallowed hard and appeared about to respond when Leary interruped.

"Detective, he's already answered you. Move on." He glanced at his watch. "I have a deposition at ten."

"You're free to go anytime you want," Gray said companionably, but Leary immediately shook his head.

"Not without my client."

"I would say that's up to him, wouldn't you?"

Leary stood up. "We're done here. Let's go, Neal." Grimm didn't move. "Neal, now."

But, Grimm shook his head. "They know a heck of a lot more than they're letting on. I'll answer their questions."

"About what?" Leary asked, surprised. He leaned close to his client and used his hand to cover his mouth, like a pitcher talking to his catcher. They whispered back and forth.

"I strongly advise you to reconsider, Neal," Leary said, dropping his hand.

"I'm a lawyer, too, Jeff," Grimm said in a soft voice. "I can handle myself."

"With all due respect, Neal, you're not a criminal attorney."

"I didn't do anything criminal," Grimm repeated more emphatically. "I told you; I can handle myself."

"I'm before Judge Carson. I can't be late."

"Then go," Grimm said. "I'll be alright."

Leary stared at him briefly, then shrugged as if to say 'suit yourself', picked up the heavy briefcase and left the room. As he was heading out the door, he stopped and turned to make one last appeal to his client, but Grimm shook his head.

"Go ahead, Jeff," he said. "I'll be fine."

Gray nodded to his partner and Kennedy produced a small digital recorder, which he placed on the table in front of Grimm, between him and Gray. Gray raised an eyebrow to Grimm, who nodded.

"Okay," Gray said, "let's cut to the chase. We know you're sleeping with Beverly." In truth, they knew no such thing; it was all conjecture based on his years of experience, but it had the desired effect. Grimm paled considerably despite his protests that he was Beverly's lawyer and nothing more.

THIRTY-THREE

Gray finally got the opportunity to check out the security footage from the bank near Big Jim's office. While he was watching, Kennedy came in and sat down.

"Anything?" he asked.

"Not yet," Gray answered, glancing at him.

"Did you see that?" Kennedy asked, leaning forward in his seat, clearly excited.

Gray turned back to the TV. "What did I miss?"

Kennedy grabbed the remote and hit 'rewind', then 'play' and Gray stood up and moved closer to the television. A car flashed past on the screen and he looked back at Kennedy and smiled.

"Well, I'll be damned," he marveled, nodding emphatically.

Kennedy jumped out of his seat. "I'll call the DA for a warrant," he said.

Now Kennedy was driving toward the house in Belle Meade. Gray sat next to him staring straight ahead, an arrest warrant in his hand, all but salivating with anticipation. It looked like the case, after so many fits and starts, had finally been broken. They pulled into the driveway and before the car had come to a full stop, he had his door open and one foot out. A marked car, driven by a female officer, followed close behind them. Phillip Butler answered their knock and looked back and forth at the grim-faced detectives.

"Can I help you, gentleman?"

"Is Mrs. Diamante at home?" Gray asked.

Phillip nodded and opened the door wider so they could enter the house.

"Yes, sir," he replied. "She is."

"Would you ask her to come to the door, please?" Kennedy asked.

Phillip said, "Of course," and turned away from them, crossed the room, and went up the grand staircase. They could hear murmured voices, one male, one female, then Beverly Diamante made her entrance. She looked extremely put upon and made no effort to hide it from the detectives. The third officer had come in right behind them and was holding her handcuffs down against her thigh.

"What is it now, detectives?" she asked, walking towards them. Apparently, she hadn't noticed the cuffs.

"Beverly Diamante," Gray said in a monotone

voice, "we have a warrant for your arrest."

She stopped dead in her tracks. "That's ridiculous," she huffed. Phillip had stopped at the bottom of the stairs and was watching the drama unfold in front of him. Kennedy glanced at him and thought he saw a small smile play across his lips.

"You'll have to come with us, ma'am," Gray continued.

She shook her head. "Like hell. Get out," she demanded, but Gray shook his head.

"I'm afraid we can't do that. We have a warrant for your arrest, duly signed by Judge Kevin King." He held it out toward her, but she slapped his hand away. He turned to the officer. "Cuff Mrs. Diamante, please."

"Get away from me!" Beverly shrieked. "You can't do this." Despite her protestations, the officer had slipped behind her and grabbed her right hand. Beverly swiped at her and the huge diamond engagement ring on her left caught the cop's cheek, drawing blood.

"Son of a bitch," Gray cursed, rushing forward. He grabbed Beverly firmly by the upper arms and forced her hands together. She was quickly restrained.

Kennedy, meanwhile, had moved close to the officer. "Are you alright?" he asked.

She swiped at the cut on her cheek, smearing blood. "I'm fine," she said through gritted teeth, glaring at Beverly.

Gray said, "Beverly Diamante, you're under arrest for the murder of James Diamante. You have the right to remain silent. Anything you say can and will be used against you in a court of law. You have the right to an attorney." At this point, Beverly came completely unhinged, screaming obscenities and threats and trying to kick anyone within reach. As Kennedy moved closer, her foot connected with his knee, eliciting a pained grunt from him. Her carefully arranged hair came loose and half-covered her face, making her look like a savage.

"And now we can add two counts of assaulting an officer," Gray concluded.

"Phillip!" she screamed, "call Neal Grimm immediately." Phillip moved toward the phone and his employer turned on Gray. "I'm going straight to Chief Wall. You sons of bitches will be lucky to wind up crossing kids on their way home from school." Gray, who had tired of her theatrics, grabbed her by the arm and half-pushed, half-dragged her toward the door.

Once she was in the car and the door was closed, Kennedy turned to Gray. "The chief is going to love this," he smiled wryly.

"Hey, her car being in the vicinity right around the time Copeland says someone entered the office speaks volumes, especially after she swore she wasn't anywhere near there. The chief can kiss my ass." The uniformed officer approached them.

"You're still bleeding," Kennedy observed. "You need to get that taken care of."

"I'm fine," the officer insisted for the second time, but Kennedy shook his head.

"No, you're not. You might need stitches. Go over to Vandy ER." The cop leaned down and looked at herself in the side view mirror on the detectives' car.

"Okay," she agreed. "I'm going." Gray climbed into the car and Kennedy slid in behind the wheel and started the car.

"Look, guys," Beverly said, trying a different tact.

"We can work something out, can't we?"

Gray turned around to look at her, incredulous. "This isn't a traffic ticket," he said. "You're being charged with murder." He turned to face forward, then turned back and added, "But, I wouldn't have given you a break on a ticket, either."

"Bastard," Beverly growled. "You won't get away with this." When he didn't respond, she said, "Martin will have your ass on a platter." Gray ignored her again and, after a few choice words and a couple more threats, she gave up.

When they arrived at police headquarters and walked Beverly into an interrogation room, Neal Grimm was waiting for them with a woman neither of the detectives knew. It was the woman who approached Beverly, not Grimm.

"Beverly, I'm Daria Cole. I'll be representing you at Mr. Grimm's request."

Beverly turned to look at Grimm. "Why aren't you representing me?" she asked, tears coming to her eyes.

Grimm put a hand on her shoulder. "Daria is one of the top criminal attorneys in the state. You'll be in good hands."

Cole looked at the detectives. "Now, if you gentleman will excuse us, I'd like to speak to my client before you begin your inquisition." She smiled smugly.

THIRTY-FOUR

"You can't do that."

"Oh, honey, I can and I will. You can take that right to the bank."

"I'm the God damned Chief of Detectives and a highly-decorated officer. Are you really naive enough to think anyone will believe you over me? You're just some bimbo who happened to turn an old man's head." Martin Wall laughed at Beverly's reaction to the insult. "Get out of my office before I have you thrown in a cell." When she didn't move, the chief bristled, "Now, Beverly. I'm not screwing around."

Beverly Diamante, fresh from questioning, during which her attorney forbade her from speaking, smiled, but it was a cold smile, so unlike the one she had used to seduce dozens of men, dozens of men whom she effortlessly convinced to do her bidding. Men like Chief of Detectives Martin Wall. But, she wasn't ready to leave just yet. She reached into her purse and, when she withdrew her hand, she was holding a small compact disc. The color immediately drained from the chief's face, while she savored the moment.

"Don't worry, Marty," she said teasingly. "I got your good side. You know, when you *were* screwing around. You should know better than anyone that Jim wasn't the only old man whose head I turned." Wall closed his eyes briefly, trying to think of a way –any way- to get out of the bind he was in. He rubbed his face, then stared at her.

"What, you have cameras in your bedroom?" he asked, disgusted and incredulous at the same time. She nodded. "You're a whore."

Beverly smiled at him. "Oh, Marty, why are you being so mean to me? You certainly didn't think ill of me when I was riding…"

"Shut up," the chief demanded. "Just shut the hell up." Then, in a much quieter voice, he asked, "What do you want?"

Beverly gave him a satisfied smirk and sat down in one of the chairs facing his desk. "My, my," she said. "You certainly have won a lot of awards." She was glancing around the office. "Oh, now that's impressive: Man of the Year from the Support of Marriage Coalition. Whatever would they say if this disc were made available to them? Or the Catholic Bishop's Conference? Man of the Year from them, too, I see. Congratulations."

Wall was seething, his face beginning to turn dark red. Veins in his temple were throbbing and he kept running a hand across his bald head, which was covered with a sheen of sweat. "Just tell me what you want." When she finished, he shook his head. "You crazy bitch. I'm not going to do that."

"Um, actually, Marty, you are. Or this," she waved the disc back and forth like a second-rate hypnotist, "goes public. I'm afraid you'll lose everything; your job, your wife, everything you care about."

Wall stood up and Beverly jumped out of her chair and took a step toward the door.

"Let me tell you something, you bitch," he said in a harsh whisper. "There's a much better chance of you winding up in a dumpster than me doing what you want. Am I making myself clear?"

She had taken two more steps toward the door and put her hand on the knob. "Go ahead," she challenged in a voice that had developed a slight tremor. "You do that, Martin. There's a copy of this in a safe deposit box, along with a letter saying that, if anything should happen to me, they should consider you the prime suspect." That said, she pulled the door open and fled the office, leaving the chief staring at the empty doorway. After several minutes, he sat back down, then immediately stood up and walked to the door.

He poked his head out. "If anybody needs me, call my cell," he said in a quiet voice.

"Yes, chief," the secretary said.

Wall started to leave, then looked back and studied the young officer sitting at the desk. "Where's Gladys?" he asked, frowning, his eyes narrowing.

"She went home early," the officer responded. "She wasn't feeling well.

This seemed to satisfy the chief, who nodded slowly. "Fine," he said. "I'm going to be out all afternoon."

"Yes, Chief," she said again. Wall grabbed his uniform hat off the coat tree next to the door and crossed the office, slipping out the back entrance. He stepped into the service elevator right across the hall that would take him down to street level.

Back in the outer office, the officer at Gladys Hilliard's desk raised the phone receiver to her ear and punched in a three-digit extension.

"Detectives, Sergeant Mitchell," a woman answered.

"Carly, it's Michelle. I need to speak to Henry Gray," she said. "It's urgent."

THIRTY-FIVE

The detectives were filling Captain Paulson in on Beverly's interview, not that it had accomplished anything, when Gray's phone rang.

"Gray. On our way." He looked at his partner, an excited smile on his face. "Our luck may be changing, buddy. A gun just turned up. A twenty-two."

"Excellent," Paulson said.

"No kidding?" Kennedy asked. "Where?"

Gray had a satisfied smile on his face. "In a dumpster around the corner from Diamante's office. At that little Italian place."

Kennedy whistled. "That's less than a quarter mile from our crime scene."

"Yep. Now we just need Beverly's prints on it."

"Good luck," Paulson said. "Go."

As they rushed out to their car, Kennedy asked, "How'd they find it?"

"You're not going to believe this," Gray said. "A homeless guy was dumpster diving and came across it. He traded it to a cook's assistant in the restaurant for some pasta. The cook's assistant got spooked when someone told him there had been a shooting nearby and threw it back in. Another employee saw him and flagged down a patrol car.

Kennedy laughed. "Well," he joked, "that was simple and straightforward." Then his smile faded. "Lots of prints."

"Yeah," Gray agreed.

Five minutes later, they pulled up in front of Scungilli's, a trendy new Italian place that catered to the college crowd. The stucco walls, checkered tablecloths, and candles in wine bottles were some designer's vision of what an authentic Italian eatery looked like. A designer who had never been to Italy and apparently had based it on what every other Italian restaurant in the States looked like. It was located midway between Diamond in the Rough and Belmont University, about a quarter mile from each. Kennedy double-parked in front of the busy restaurant. There were white Christmas-style lights strung in the trees on the sidewalk and dozens of people, all young and all with drinks in their hands, were milling about watching the officers. A patrolman was there to keep anyone from trying to go behind the building, where other personnel were standing around and talking, waiting for the detectives to show up. Kennedy and Gray got out and walked to the small parking lot in the back. Two techs from the crime scene unit were standing next to a battered blue dumpster, smoking. They nodded at the two detectives.

"You've got a gun for us?" Gray asked.

One of the men reached into a container that was sitting between his feet and produced a small pistol inside a plastic bag marked "Evidence". The date, time, and location of its discovery were carefully written on the bag's label. The man held the bag by a corner and handed it to Gray.

"Here you go, detective. It's a twenty-two. It's been fired recently but wasn't cleaned after."

Gray examined the gun through the bag, then handed it back. "Make sure that gets to the lab right away," he said.

"Absolutely," the tech said. "That's your murder weapon right there."

"From your mouth to God's ear," Gray said, nodding.

"What can I tell you? I'm a positive thinker." He smiled and Gray returned it.

He clapped the man on the back. "Thanks," he said. He and Kennedy walked quickly back to their car.

A pretty young woman wearing a Belmont shirt tied in a knot above her flat, pierced belly eyed them as they passed. "I love cops," she said, smiling in a way that they surmised was supposed to pass for seductive.

Gray regarded her coolly. "You look awfully young to be drinking," he said. "Maybe I should check your ID?"

The woman looked flustered, then recovered

quickly and retorted, "Well, not *all* cops." She turned away, flipping her hair as she did and sauntered back into the restaurant.

Gray shook his head and looked at his partner, who was smiling at him. "What?" he asked.

"You enjoyed that, didn't you?" Kennedy laughed.

Gray considered that for a moment, then smiled and nodded. "Actually, I did."

THIRTY-SIX

The detectives were about to call it a day when Kennedy suddenly said, "Here we go." He was looking past Gray, toward the door to the detectives' squad room. Gray heard a commotion behind him and turned to see what was going on. Chief Wall was storming in with a full head of steam, his face almost purple, and he was making a beeline straight toward them.

"Are you a complete idiot or just incompetent?" he yelled, stopping next to Gray's desk and glaring down at him. "I told you to handle Bev Diamante with kid gloves and this is how you do it?" Henry, who would later realize that this was his watershed moment, the exact instant he decided he was retiring, stood up and got nose-to-nose with Wall.

"Your doer is Wheeler." Wall seethed. "Do I need to write that down for you, Detective?"

"I know what I'm doing," he said, "and I don't need you meddling in my case. And I sure as hell don't need you dressing me down like this in front of the whole squad."

Wall thrust a finger in the detective's face. "I run this unit, not you. Don't you forget that. When I tell you how I want something handled, you damn well better do it that way. Now back the fuck off Beverly Diamante."

"You want to take the case?" Henry challenged; hands thrown out to his sides, his eyes flashing with anger. He turned, grabbed a folder off his desk, and shoved it at the chief. "Fine. Knock yourself out." Captain Paulson came rushing out of his office, crossed the room quickly, and wedged himself between the two men. Kennedy, meanwhile, had grabbed Gray from behind in a bear hug and was trying to drag him away.

"You're insubordinate. I want this man off the case," Wall demanded, turning his fury on the captain.

"Why don't we go in my office, Chief?" Paulson suggested, but Wall shook his head.

"No. He's off the case. End of story." He turned away and then spun back to face Gray. "In fact, you're all done here," he said. "Clean out your desk." He turned away and stalked out of the room as abruptly as he'd come in.

"What the hell was that all about?" Paulson asked Kennedy, who shook his head and shrugged. "Come on, both of you." He turned and walked toward his office. As soon as they were inside, he shut the door, then went and sat behind his cluttered desk.

"What was that?" he asked. He didn't sound angry, but, rather, perplexed. Gray, who was still seething, glared at him but didn't respond. "What are you pissed at me for?" Paulson asked. Gray pulled down his tie and undid the top button of his shirt, but remained silent. He still looked like he wanted to punch a hole in the wall, so Kennedy spoke up. When he finished telling the story of their visit to the Diamante house, Paulson rolled his eyes, then his neck, then rubbed at his face with both hands. He blew out a breath.

"If you guys had it to do again, would you approach it the same way?" he asked, finally.

"Yeah," Kennedy said immediately. "He told us he suspected her anyway and her car was right near the office around the time Big Jim was killed."

Paulson looked at Gray, who was facing away from him, staring out the window. "Henry?"

Gray didn't turn around. "Yeah, I'd do it the same way again. And the next time and the time after that."

"Okay," the captain said. "Get back to it."

"What about the chief?" Kennedy asked.

"Fuck him," Gray snapped.

Paulson glanced at him but ignored the comment. "I'll give him a little time to cool off and then I'll go up and talk to him. Just do what you need to do." Then he added, "And you take a little time to cool off, too," but Gray didn't acknowledge him, just stalked out of the office.

The captain looked at Kennedy. "Go get coffee or something. Let him cool his jets for a bit."

Everyone in the squad room watched Gray go to his desk, wondering what had just transpired; if he had really just been fired.

"You guys got nothing better to do?" Kennedy barked as soon as he walked out of the captain's office. Everyone immediately found something interesting on their desk and stopped watching Gray.

THIRTY-SEVEN

Despite the chief's threats, Beverly Diamante had been brought before the Grand Jury as the District Attorney's office sought to indict her for her husband's murder. Lead Prosecutor Brodie Lane stood up and walked toward the witness stand, where she was sitting with her hands folded in her lap. It seemed as if everyone in the courtroom was holding their breath.

"Now, Mrs. Diamante, did you go to your husband's office on the day he was killed?"

Beverly, who looked stunning in her mourning ensemble, tossed her hair before responding.

"I avoided the office," she sniffed. "That was Jim's place."

"So, you weren't there that day?"

"As I believe I just told you, Mr. Lane," she said, putting on a dismissive air, as if these proceedings were beneath her. Now and then she dabbed at her eyes with an embroidered handkerchief, playing the grieving widow to the hilt, but being careful not to smudge her makeup. She knew the TV cameras would be in front of the courthouse when she made her exit. "I avoided the office," she said again.

"I see," Lane said. "Tell me, Mrs. Diamante, what kind of car do you drive?" Beverly looked rattled by the question and finally fastened her wide eyes on her lawyer. Her expression pleaded, what do I do now? But the lawyer just stared back at her. By law, there wasn't much more she could do. This was a grand jury hearing, after all, not a trial. The rules were quite different. "Mrs. Diamante?"

Beverly looked back at Lane. "Hmm?" It was clear she was stalling for time, trying to figure out where Lane was heading with this line of questioning. It seemed to her to have come completely out of left field, although it was a pretty straightforward question.

"Mrs. Diamante?" Lane said. "I must remind you that you're under oath and expected to answer my questions.

She looked at Daria Cole again, who nodded and mouthed a single word, 'Answer'.

Beverly licked her lips. "A Corvette," she responded.

"Could you please be a bit more specific?" Lane asked.

"A nineteen-sixty-three Corvette," she said, finally.

"A nineteen-sixty-three Corvette," Lane repeated. "Nice ride." He smiled at her.

"Uh, thank you?" Beverly said uncertainly. There was a ripple of laughter from the jurors and spectators alike.

Lane nodded to her and favored her with a warm smile. "So, a sixty-three Corvette. Yessirree, that is a nice automobile. I always wanted one of those. Say, what color is yours?" Lane had let his southern accent thicken slightly.

"What?"

"I asked you what color your car is?"

"Um…"

"Did you forget, Mrs. Diamante?" Another ripple of laugher.

"Yellow."

"Yellow," Lane repeated, nodding. "Hmm, that car was never manufactured in yellow. Did you know that? I wonder how many yellow, nineteen sixty-three Corvettes there are tooling around Nashville? Would you care to venture a guess?" He smiled at Beverly again as if they were friends sharing pleasant conversation over a cup of coffee. She was just starting back at him, her pretty mouth forming a ripe, red 'o'. Daria Cole was sitting off to the side with a look of utter resignation on her face.

"Mrs. Diamante," Lane continued, "how many yellow, nineteen-sixty-three Corvettes do you think there are in the metro Nashville area?

"Well, I don't know," Beverly answered, seeming quite frazzled. "Ten?" Her eyes had taken on a wild look; like that of a captured animal.

"Ten?" Lane said, feigning surprise. "Ten? Is

that your final answer?" More laughter.

"Mr. Lane!" Ms. Cole snapped, getting to her feet.

"My apologies, Ms. Cole." He turned his attention back to Beverly. "Would it surprise you, Mrs. Diamante, to know there's a grand total of one? Yours." Beverly didn't respond, just kept trying to make eye contact with her lawyer, who was looking at the jurors. All twenty-three of them were watching Lane and Beverly raptly. Lane walked over to a video monitor on a rolling cart. Under the monitor was a DVD player. He pushed a button, and a yellow Corvette appeared on the screen.

"This is the footage from the drive-thru camera at the Sun Trust bank branch located two doors down and across the street from Diamond in the Rough Publishing. It's pointed out toward Grand Avenue. As you can see, a yellow Corvette goes by the bank, heading left to right on the screen, so in the direction of Big Jim's office. If you look at the time and date stamp in the corner," he pointed, just in case anyone missed it, "you can see this yellow Corvette going by on the very day Jim Diamante was shot to death, roughly five minutes before the shooting." He hit a button to make the DVD fast forward. "And here's the same car going in the opposite direction, about eight minutes later, just after Mr. Diamante was killed. So, if you never went to the office, why was your car there?" He shut the DVD player off, then the TV, and then turned to face the jurors, although he was still speaking to Beverly.

"Well, Mrs. Diamante?" he asked, his voice rising. "Do you have any explanation as to why your car was in that area?"

"I, well, I, um, well, no. I mean, someone must

have taken it without my knowledge," she stammered.

Lane strode toward her, talking as he did, his voice rising in volume. "And this person just happened to be in the vicinity of your husband's office right around the time he was killed? Don't you find that just a little bit coincidental?

"I object to this line of questioning, Mr. Lane!" Cole said. "My client already said she wasn't there, and someone else must have been driving her car, someone who took her car without her permission."

Lane turned on her. "You're out of order, Ms. Cole," he said sternly. "May I remind you that you're here as a courtesy? You can keep your comments to yourself, or I'll have you removed."

He spun back toward Beverly. "Mrs. Diamante, are you stating, *under oath*, that you were not driving your yellow, nineteen-sixty-three Corvette on the date in question, at the time in question? Is that your testimony?

"Asked and answered," Cole almost shouted. Lane turned quickly and strode back to where his assistant was holding what appeared to be a photograph. He took it from her and walked back to the witness stand.

"This is a still photo taken from the video we just saw, enlarged, that clearly shows you driving your car in the bank footage in question. There is absolutely no doubt that it's your car, nor is there any doubt you're driving." Lane walked to the jury box and handed the photo to the person on the left front end, instructing her to pass it to her left after she took a good look, so everyone could see it.

Beverly watched this, wide-eyed while her lawyer

stared at her.

THIRTY-EIGHT

Kennedy was at a parole board hearing for a man he had arrested years earlier, before he made detective. Gray had just returned from the men's room and was sitting at his desk, going over their notes for the hundredth time.

"Henry."

He swiveled his chair and looked up to see Paulson standing in the doorway to his office, a deep frown on his face. He hadn't recognized the captain's voice; it sounded choked with emotion. Gray got up and quickly crossed the room, wondering what else could go wrong. When he got to the office, Paulson stepped to one side to allow him to enter.

As soon as he went in, Gray pulled up short. "What's he doing here?" he asked, clearly taken aback. There was a tall, heavyset man black man with a gray crew cut watching him carefully. His gold shield was hanging on a chain around his neck.

Paulson stepped all the way in and shut the door. "Sit down, Henry," he said. "Detective Renfro has something to discuss with us." Marcus Renfro was a member of the department's Internal Affairs Bureau, or IAB. Henry didn't trust IAB, nor did anyone he knew. In fact, they were almost universally referred to as "the rat squad" by the rank and file. An IAB officer's job was to investigate complaints and criminal charges against police officers who were unfortunate –or stupid- enough to show up on their radar. Gray had had a couple of run-ins over the years with IAB in general and Renfro, in particular. In fact, the last time had been in reference to Sonny Munson's dislocated shoulder and just what part Gray had played in it. There was no love lost between the two officers.

Gray sat down in one of the chairs facing the captain's desk. Renfro was sitting behind the desk, and Paulson was standing off to one side, near the window. Outside, it had started to rain lightly. Most of the drivers had switched their headlights on. Gray looked back and forth between the two men.

"Well?" he asked, finally. Paulson nodded to Renfro, who opened a manila folder and pulled out a picture, which he slid across the desk to Gray. It was a surveillance photo of a known prostitute and-presumably-a customer. Gray glanced at it, then pushed it back across the desk.

"So?" he said. Renfro removed another photo and

slid that one across the desk. Gray picked this picture up and looked at it. It was the same prostitute as in the previous image, sitting in the same car, except in the first one the man had his head turned away from the camera. In this one, Gray could clearly see that the man resembled him. Gray stared wordlessly at the picture for a moment, then half slid, half threw the photo back at Renfro and smiled.

"If you trying to say that's me, you're out of your mind."

"I didn't say it was you, Detective," Renfro replied in measured tones, "although it's interesting to me how quickly *you* went there." He sat back and eyed Gray.

"And even if it was me," Gray said, "I'm a detective. I interview suspects and witnesses all the time." He glared at the IAB man.

Renfro nodded, then produced a third shot. "So I guess in this one she's talking into your microphone?" In the picture, the man –Gray, presumably; his face was turned away again- was leaning back against his seat and the prostitute was bent over with her head in his lap.

Gray didn't touch this picture, just stood up. "Fuck you," he swore at Renfro, then walked toward the door.

"Henry," Paulson began.

Gray turned on him. "If you're buying this shit, fuck you, too," he spat and stormed out of the office. Paulson let him go.

"Still a hothead, huh?" Renfro commented, his tone smug. "I would have hoped the years had mellowed him. You're going to let him get away with that?"

Paulson studied him for a few moments, then said, "You're going to tell me how to run my squad, Renfro? Get the hell out of my office." Renfro gathered his pictures and slipped them into his folder, then stood up.

"This isn't going away, Captain," he warned. He dropped the folder back onto the desktop. "You can keep these," he said. "I have copies."

"Get out," Paulson repeated, taking a step toward him, "before I throw you out."

"Do I need to remind you you're obligated to cooperate fully with my investigation, Captain?" Renfro asked, his tone icy.

"You're leaving," Paulson said. "Now. Out the door or the window, it's your choice."

Renfro stopped in the doorway. "You can threaten me all you want, Captain, but this isn't going away," he said.

"Dismissed," Paulson said, which gave Renfro no choice but to walk away.

Gray was still sitting at his desk, rubbing at his forehead, when Renfro walked by, favoring him with another smug look.

"You're enjoying this, aren't you, you bastard?" Gray said.

"Just doing my job, Detective."

"Yeah, right." As soon as he left the squad room, Gray stood up and went back into Paulson's office. The captain was standing at the window, looking down at the traffic on Broadway. Or perhaps at nothing at all. When he continued to stare out, Gray cleared his throat. Paulson turned around, his face somber.

"This is bad, Henry."

"It's not me," Henry insisted, but even to himself, his words sounded both hollow and defensive. When Paulson didn't respond, he grew angry and said, "How long have you known me, captain?"

"Long enough to give you the benefit of the doubt," Paulson said. "But, it's not me you need to convince, it's the brass. The chief is just looking for a reason to stick a hot poker up your ass."

"Someone's setting me up," Henry insisted. "That picture had to be photo-shopped. Beverly goes before the grand jury and, all of a sudden, IAB is looking at me?"

"Do you know the pro?" Paulson asked.

"Yeah, Jeanette Lewis. She's one of the regulars around Trinity Lane. I've questioned her in relation to a few cases over the past couple years. She's pretty reliable. If she's saying I did anything like that, I don't know where it's coming from. Unless someone put her up to it."

"She's been in your car?"

"Yeah, just like three-quarters of the people I interview."

"Where was Kennedy?"

"Jesus Christ," Gray exploded. "Do I need my PBA rep?"

"Henry, I'm on your side, but Renfro claims to have a statement from the woman in the photo saying it's exactly what it looks like. And that it wasn't the first time."

Gray dropped heavily into a chair. "I don't believe this. I'm telling you, that photo was played around with. The first two look legit, but the third one is pure fiction."

"Okay, Henry, Paulson said finally. "But, as a friend, I'd advise you to get that rep. I doubt the boys upstairs are going to take your word for it like I do." Gray stood and walked toward to the door. "Where do you think you're going?" Paulson asked.

"To talk to Jeanette."

"I don't think so," Paulson replied. "You're not going anywhere near her. Understood?"

Gray turned around. "I have to talk to her," he insisted.

"You're the last person who should be anywhere near her. How do you think that would play upstairs?"

"So what am I supposed to do? Just sit on my ass and wait for the other shoe to fall?"

"I'll send someone out there. Where's Peyton."

"Peyton's an asshole," Gray protested.

"And?"

"And you're going to send an asshole who hates my guts out there to clear me?"

Paulson considered this for a moment. "Fine. I'll talk to her," he said.

Gray looked at him questioningly. "Since when do they let COs go out on the street?" he asked.

"Since I said so," Paulson responded. "The more I think about it, the more I'd prefer to keep everyone besides us out of this particular loop anyway."

Gray thought about that for a moment, then nodded. "I got you, Captain. Thanks."

Paulson took his suit jacket off a rack near the door. "Get back to work on the Diamond mess and I'll go find the girl.

THIRTY-NINE

West Trinity Lane is about three miles from the heart of downtown Nashville, hard off the Interstate, but it might as well be on the far side of the moon, atmosphere-wise. A few 'no-tell motels' cater to the scores of songwriters who arrive in town each day hoping to become 'The Next Big Thing' in the music business and can't afford nicer digs closer to downtown and Music Row, as well as to married guys who don't care to spend too much money on a love shack. The cabbies in the city know that, if their fare is looking for a little something to get them through the long, dark night, be it pharmaceuticals or companionship, this is the place to bring them.

It didn't take long for Paulson to find Jeanette, who was hanging out at a nearby Waffle House, drinking coffee and chain-smoking Marlboros. It looked like she had been there for a while; there were at least a dozen lipstick-ringed cigarette butts in the overflowing ashtray on the table in front of her. Paulson had looked up her sheet before he left his office, so he knew she was thirty-five but, up close, he would have sworn she was in her fifties. She had the look of someone who had started off very attractive and drugged and drank herself into her current state. Her hair hung to her shoulders in a tangled mess, her complexion was sallow and lined, and her clothes looked like something the Salvation Army would have turned down had she tried to donate them. He walked to where she was sitting and slid into the other side of the booth, which prompted her to start to get up.

"Sit back down and listen, Jeanette," Paulson instructed. She stopped halfway to standing and squinted at him through a veil of cigarette smoke. After weighing her options, she dropped back onto the well-worn cushion.

"Do I know you?" she asked. She looked at him carefully, then shook her head. "I know all the cops, so who are you?"

"How do you know I'm a cop?" Paulson asked.

"You've got the look," Jeanette replied. "And the smell," she added, wrinkling her nose. "What do you want?" Paulson was carrying the folder the pictures Renfro had left with him were in. He slipped out the first one, the one in which it the man was turned away from the camera, and placed it on the table between them.

"Is this you?" he asked. Even though he knew the answer, he wanted her to confirm it.

Jeanette looked at it briefly, then shrugged. "Could be."

Paulson pulled out the next picture and put it down. "How about this?"

Jeanette started to stand up again. This time, Paulson grabbed her by the wrist.

"Sit down," he ordered. When she didn't, he added, "Relax. I'm not Vice."

She eyed him suspiciously. "Then who are you?" she asked finally.

"Homicide." That single word seemed to send Jeanette into a panic, and she tried to leave a third time, but Paulson was still holding her wrist.

"Now, wait a minute," she protested, her eyes getting comically wide. "I don't know anything about a homicide."

Paulson increased the pressure on her wrist, not enough to hurt, but enough to let her know she wasn't going anywhere until he said so.

"Sit down," he said in a soft voice. He felt eyes on them and glanced around. Two college-aged guys were watching them from a booth on the opposite side of the dining room. One of them was pointing his cell phone at them. Paulson stared at him, and he looked back defiantly, but then put the phone on the table and dropped his eyes. Paulson turned back to Jeanette, who was fidgeting with her pack of smokes.

"We can do this here or at the station," he said. She stopped struggling and settled back into her seat. As soon as Paulson let go of her wrist, she lit a new cigarette with the one she was currently smoking.

Paulson took out the third picture and laid it on the table. This time, instead of looking at it, Jeanette turned her head toward the wall.

Paulson tapped the picture with one long finger. "Look at it, Jeanette. You?"

She nodded. "So what if it is?"

"Who's the customer?" Jeanette shrugged. "Is it the same guy as the other two pictures?"

"Looks like," she said, "so it must be. Can I go now?"

"We're not done." The woman slumped further into her seat. "We both know who the man in the first two pictures is. What I want to know is, is the same man in the third picture?"

Suddenly, Jeanette smiled and Paulson did a double-take. Her teeth were beautiful, a stark contrast to the rest of her appearance. It took him a moment to realize they were false.

"I get it," she said. "You're looking for some of that for yourself, aren't you, sweetie? That's why we're sitting here, huh? I could throw you a freebie now and then if you want."

Paulson shook his head. "I told you why I'm here, Jeanette. If you think offering me a bribe is in your best interest, you're nuts."

Jeanette held her hands up to him, palms out. "Slow down, honey. I'm not offering you a bribe.

"No?" Paulson countered. "Freebie, bribe, it's all the same thing. Trust me, you don't want me for an enemy."

Jeanette shook her head, and her shoulders slumped. "I'm not looking for trouble," she said dully.

"Then answer the damn question. Is it the same

man in all three pictures or not?"

Jeanette looked around as if she were expecting someone to come rushing into the restaurant and rescue her. Finally, resigned, she shook her head.

"It's the same guy, but it's not his face. I mean, it's not who you think it is."

"What? Who put you up to this?" Paulson asked.

"I can't," Jeanette said, shaking her head, her eyes wide with fear.

"You better or I'm going to take you in right now," he said.

"Please," she begged, tears starting to stream down her cheeks. Just then, Paulson caught movement from the corner of his eye. Before he could turn toward it, someone had grabbed him by the shoulder and was yanking him up out of his seat.

"Leave her alone, dude. She's not interested." Paulson realized that his assailant was the same guy who had been videotaping them with his phone earlier. The man suddenly swung at him. Paulson grabbed his wrist and, before the would-be hero knew what was happening, his arm had been twisted behind his back, causing him to howl in pain.

As soon as that happened, the man who had been sitting with him wrapped Paulson up in a bear hug. The first man managed to elbow him in the stomach, knocking the wind out of him. Paulson sagged, but he still had hold of the man's other arm and used all his strength to twist it viciously.

"I'm a cop, you stupid bastards," he managed. The man who was hugging him let go and Paulson slid most of the way to the floor before he was able to regain his feet. The two men looked terrified. "You stupid bastards," he repeated, then glanced around. "Shit!" he yelled, hitting the table hard enough to tip over the salt and pepper shakers. Jeanette was gone. She had used the attack as a distraction and was in the wind.

"You," Paulson shouted at the cook, who had stood by and watched the men attack him without intervening. "Where did she go?" The man shrugged, which angered the captain further. "You just witnessed an assault on a police officer and stood there with your thumb up your ass. Now tell me where she went, or I'll bring you in."

This time, the man pointed with his spatula. "Out the door. She usually works the corner near the laundry." Paulson raced outside.

He had driven around for twenty minutes before he spotted Jeanette a block away from where the cook told him to look for her. He glided up to the curb, and she walked up to the open passenger window.

"Hey, baby, want to party?" she asked as she leaned into the window. When she realized who was in the car, she recoiled. "Oh, shit. Just leave me alone."

"Listen to me, Jeanette. If I bring you in on a prostitution charge, a judge will take one look at your sheet and throw you in jail. Then he'll drop the key in the ocean. Is that what you want?"

Jeanette knew it was over. "What do you want to know?"

"You gave a statement that just might ruin a great cop's career. Who put you up to it?"

FORTY

The day of his murder, Beverly Diamante had stormed into Big Jim's office spoiling for a fight. Jim leaned back in the chair, holding the phone away from his ear.

"What are you doing here?" he asked, annoyed.

"I just tried to use my platinum card at Ross-Simons and guess what happened?" Jim smiled but didn't respond. Instead, he leaned back in his chair and put his free hand behind his head. "You bastard," she fumed. "You shut me off. Do you know how humiliating that was for me?" Just then, Beverly glanced down and saw a gun on the corner of her husband's desk. Without thinking, she reached down and grabbed it. "Maybe I should blow your head off, you son of a bitch."

Jim sat up straight and raised his free hand in a warding off gesture. He was still smiling, but the expression seemed frozen on his face. His eyes were full of fear.

"Now, you don't want to do that," he said and started to get up, then stopped halfway with the receiver held against his chest. They stayed like that, staring at one another, for several tense seconds. Then, without warning, Beverly pulled the trigger. It may be that she didn't even realize she was doing it; she seemed startled when the first shot rang out. A look of utter shock appeared on Jim's face and he fell back down into his chair, reaching for his upper arm. The bullet had pierced just below his left shoulder and must have gone clean through him because Beverly saw a little puff of plaster dust as it buried itself in the wall. Suddenly, it was like everything was happening in both high definition and slow motion. Beads of sweat popped out on Jim's forehead, then slowly trickled down. She fired again, and again; five more shots in all. Jim's body jumped in his chair like a fish on a hook. His head snapped back and hit the back of the chair, knocking his trademark hat off his head. It tumbled to the floor and landed upside down. She continued pulling the trigger, but now the gun just clicked. Blood had spattered on the wall and pictures behind the desk Beverly was panting, and on the verge of panic as she began to back out of the office, ears ringing. The air was hazy with smoke.

At some point, she dropped the gun without noticing, because, when she finally looked down, her hand was empty. She ran out to her car, but just sat in the parking lot, trying to figure out what to do next.

It suddenly occurred to her that, if she got out of there quickly, no one could tie her to the murder. She'd be 'poor Beverly, Big Jim's grieving widow' and his entire fortune, less what he left to that snotty bitch of a daughter, would be hers. She started the 'Vette and drove off, screeching the tires in her haste. As she drove, she tried desperately to formulate her alibi, then pushed a button on the car's dash.

"Call Neal Grimm," she said aloud.

A mechanical voice responded immediately. "Calling Neal Grimm." After two rings, Grimm's secretary answered the phone.

"It's Beverly Diamante. I need to speak to Mr. Grimm right away."

"I'm sorry," the secretary responded. "Mr. Grimm is unavailable at the moment."

"Well, make him available," Beverly said through clenched teeth.

"I'm sorry, Mrs. Diamante…"

Beverly didn't let her finish her thought. "You listen to me," she said, "I need to speak to Neal right now. Get him on the god dammed phone. Now!"

The secretary who, after twenty years was used to being verbally abused by clients, took a breath and said, "As I'm trying to explain to you, Mrs. Diamante, Mr. Grimm is not in the office. May I…"

"Stupid bitch," Beverly snapped and disconnected the call. "Neal Grimm cell," she told the car phone. He picked up on the fourth ring.

"Beverly, how are you?" he said. She could hear

the smile in his voice and knew he was thinking this call might lead to them winding up in bed together. He was so easy to read. Like most men, she had found.

"Neal, I need your help," she said.

"Oh, I'm sure I can figure out some way to help you, Miss Beverly," he purred.

"Neal, I'm not kidding, I need your help."

Now he caught on to the urgency in her voice. "What's wrong?" he asked, then held the phone away from his mouth. "Go ahead, guys," he called. "I'll catch up with you."

"Where are you?" Beverly demanded.

"I'm at Hermitage playing nine holes. Why? What's going on?"

One of his friends had walked over to him. "We'll leave a cart for you," he said. Neal nodded impatiently and waved him off.

"There's a problem," Beverly said.

"What?"

"Jim's been shot."

Grimm's jaw dropped and the golf club he was holding fell from his hand. It clattered to the concrete walkway he was standing on, causing his friend to turn around and look at him questioningly. He took a step toward him and Grimm waved him off again.

"Tell me what happened."

"He cut me off, that's what happened," she hissed.

"What? What do you mean, he cut you…?" Recognition dawned in his eyes. "Wait. He cut you off *and you shot him?* Oh, my God. Beverly, what were you thinking? How could you do that?" He slapped a hand against his forehead and slumped against a post he happened to be next to, not believing what she was telling him. Two men walked by, slowing down and watching him curiously, but Grimm glared at them and they continued on their way.

"I didn't mean to," Beverly whined, and he could tell she was on the verge of tears. He knew if he didn't take charge of the situation immediately, she'd fall apart and he'd never get the details."

"Get hold of yourself, Beverly," he said sharply. "Where are you?"

"In the car."

"Are you driving?"

"No, I'm pulled over."

"Okay," Grimm said. "Good. Now, start from the beginning and tell me what happened." Beverly related the story quickly as Grimm stood there rubbing the bridge of his nose. As an officer of the court, he had an obligation to report this at once, but as Beverly's lover, he couldn't imagine turning her in.

"Do you still have the gun?"

"No."

"Where is it?"

"I don't know."

"Think. Did you leave it in the office?"

"I...I guess. I don't know." She was crying now, barely holding it together.

He thought feverishly. Then an idea occurred to him. "Beverly, listen carefully, because this is very important. Go home and stay there and, for God's sake, don't talk to anyone. I have to make a call." He disconnected without saying goodbye, the dialed a number.

When a man answered, Grimm said, "Don't talk, just listen. I need you to take care of something." He told him what he wanted him to do.

Finally, after a moment of silence, the man said, "No, I won't do that. I can't."

"Listen to me," Grimm said. "You do this for me and that other thing goes away. Permanently."

FORTY-ONE

Gray and Kennedy were sitting in a sports bar that had just opened. Late that afternoon, the Grand Jury had returned an indictment against Beverly Diamante for murder and they were celebrating. The bar was one of those places that seem to have two huge televisions per patron to show every game in whatever sport is in season, but was so noisy you can't hear the announcers. Over in one corner, a boisterous, obviously-drunken group of young men playing darts was hooting and yelling at every wildly missed shot. Gray thought maybe someone needed to take the darts away from them before they had their first casualty of the night. They had just ordered a round when Gray took his phone out of his jacket pocket.

"Sheila," he mouthed to his partner. Sheila Reynolds was the Medical Examiner they usually dealt with. "Hold on," he said into the phone. "Hold on," louder. "I have to take this outside," he told Kennedy and started to make his way through the crowd. Once out on the sidewalk, he put the phone to his ear again. "Sheila? You still there?"

"Where else would I be?" she asked. "Where are you? Jeez, it's loud."

"We're at that new sports bar on Broadway."

"Oh yeah? I've been meaning to check it out, but I don't have anyone to go with. How is it?" Sheila asked.

"Loud just about covers it," Gray cracked, missing her point entirely. "What's up?" Around him, neon light seemed to pour from every storefront and people were swarming on the sidewalk; an interesting mix of college jocks and wannabe cowboys. Still, it was quieter here than inside, although just barely.

"Are you sitting down?"

"No, I just walked outside so I could hear you." A car full of young men cruised by, horn honking. They were yelling and holding beer cans out of the car windows. Gray shook his head as they rolled through a red light.

"Oh, okay. Listen, I read about the Big Jim case while I was in Dallas."

"Is that where you've been? What's in Dallas?" Gray asked.

"My mom. She fell and broke her hip a few weeks ago. I went down to stay with her."

"Oh, I'm sorry to hear that. Is she going to be

okay?"

"Yeah," Sheila replied. "She's a tough one. My sister is there now, then my other sister will take over. After that, maybe I'll go back. By then, she should be getting around pretty well with a walker."

"Damn," Gray said.

"Anyway, I read about the case, so when I got back I went through Bo's notes." Gray sensed something in her tone that said there might be a problem. "Just out of curiosity."

"Come on, Sheila, drop the other shoe already."

"When I got in this morning, I went over the photos and the full report."

"Why do I have a sinking feeling in my gut?" Gray asked. Kennedy had come outside to look for him. He spotted him halfway down the block, standing under a streetlight.

"Nice job skipping out on the tab," he joked. Gray covered the phone with his hand.

"That's not going to be the worst thing that happens to you tonight," he said. Kennedy put his head back and scanned the sky. On this bright city street, there wasn't much to see up there even though the night was clear.

"Why? What's the matter?" he asked.

"So what did you find, Sheila?"

"Hold onto your hat, Henry."

"Aw, jeez," he moaned. Kennedy was watching him closely and now he held out his hands in a gesture of supplication.

"What?" he mouthed.

Sheila told Gray what she suspected. When she was done, he thanked her and made arrangements to meet her at her office in the morning. He slipped his phone back into his pocket and looked at Kennedy.

"Sounds like Bo may have screwed the pooch on the COD," he said. Kennedy looked at him with a shocked expression.

"How?" he asked. "She shot him six times."

"Sheila doesn't think he died from the gunshot wounds."

Kennedy rubbed his forehead. "Holy Christ," he muttered. "So, there goes the indictment."

"Yep," Gray agreed. "If she's right –and she always is- it's gonna have to be amended. I'm gonna head home. She wants to meet us at the ME's office at eight so she can take a closer look and go over it with us. I guess I'll see you there." He turned and walked to where he'd parked his Harley, feeling a knot in the pit of his stomach, and threw his leg over. He pulled on his gloves, then started the engine, but he didn't drive off right away. Instead, he went over everything Sheila had just told him. Finally, he glanced over his shoulder and slipped into a break in the stream of cars going by.

All the way home, he turned this new possibility over and over in his mind. *How could someone be shot six times at close range and have something else be the cause of death?* He wondered. *And, if the gunshots didn't kill him, what did? Heart attack? Hell, I'd probably have a heart attack if someone shot me six times.* All the way home Gray pondered all of the possibilities he could imagine. As he pulled into his driveway, he saw a shadow near some hedges next to the front door. He shut the bike off, set the alarm, and climbed off. The shadow drew closer.

"Hello, young lady," he said, bending down. A

small tan and white tabby cat made its way between his feet, rubbing its head on his calves. Gray picked her up and put his nose to hers. "Ready to come inside, Samantha?" he asked. He had named her after Elizabeth Montgomery's character on the old sitcom, Bewitched because the cat had a strange habit of wrinkling and twitching her nose. Gray carried her into the house, depositing her on the kitchen counter. While she watched him, tail swishing back and forth, he opened a cabinet and took out a bag of cat treats, poured some into his hand, and walked back to her.

FORTY-TWO

The Office of the Medical Examiner occupies a long, two-story brick building four blocks from the police station. Set back off the road, it's surrounded by a sea of asphalt and a ten-foot-tall chain link fence. The architect apparently made no effort to make it attractive in any way; the brickwork is a dull, dark brown, and all the window frames and doors are battleship grey. The vans that the MEs use -one black and one dark blue- were backed up against two overhead doors marked 1 and 2. A small sign identified the building's purpose, a second warned against smoking on the premises, and a third alerted visitors and trespassers alike that the facility is monitored twenty-four, seven. If the goal was to create something utterly utilitarian and depressing, the mark was struck dead-center.

Gray drove into the parking lot at seven-fifty, and Kennedy was already there, pulled in against the building. Gray backed in next to him, so their driver's side windows were next to each other. Kennedy reached out his window with a cup of coffee.

"Thanks," Gray said, taking it from him. "I didn't sleep worth a damn last night. You?"

Kennedy shook his head. "Nah, I tossed and turned so much Jodie went out and slept on the couch." They sat in silence, sipping coffee, each lost in his own thoughts.

Finally, Kennedy asked, "What does this mean? If the gunshots didn't kill Big Jim, what did?"

"Hell if I know," Gray answered. "Here's Sheila." A silver BMW convertible had just entered the parking lot. The ME pulled in on the other side of Gray's car and got out.

"Morning, boys," she said, walking to the back of her car to wait for them. Gray got out to join her, and then Kennedy, holding a third coffee cup.

He handed it to the ME, who smiled. "Why, thank you kindly, Brett," she said.

"Welcome. You really think Bo messed up?" Kennedy asked. Sheila tipped her head toward the building.

"Oh, there's big problems with this one, but I wanted to talk to you guys before I did anything." She swiped her employee ID badge to get into the building, and they walked in single file, Gray taking up the rear. After thirty years, he hated the morgue more than ever. It wasn't the bodies; it was the smell. Even Vick's

VapoRub smeared on his upper lip wasn't enough. He had slowed markedly upon entering the building, and now he hurried to catch up.

Sheila noticed he was lagging behind a bit, and she knew why.

"Why don't we go up to the office?" she suggested, then caught Gray's eye. "The smell doesn't get all the way up there."

Gray smiled with gratitude.

The upstairs office at the morgue was much different than the detectives expected. It had several desks with computers on them, but also a homey lounge area with overstuffed sofas and armchairs. There was a large-screen TV on one wall and a large bookshelf that took up most of another and looked to be equally laden with bestsellers and medical texts. Next to that there was a full-sized refrigerator and a microwave.

"All the comforts, huh?" Gray said admiringly. "Not what I imagined at all."

"You should come around more often," Sheila said as she walked to a desk and picked up a clipboard, then crossed the room to the lounge. She dropped into a chair and motioned for the detectives to follow suit.

"Make yourselves at home," she said. She pointed to the kitchenette. "There's coffee, tea, soft drinks. Help yourself."

"I'm all set, thanks," Gray said, sitting down.

Kennedy walked over and opened the fridge, selected a can of soda, then turned around. "You sure, Henry?" he asked. "Sheila? You want anything?" They both said they didn't, so Kennedy went to sit down, popping the tab on a Pepsi as he did. He took a long swallow, then put his hand over his mouth to stifle a soundless belch.

"I went over Bo's notes for the tenth time last night," Sheila started, "and I honestly don't see any way any of the six shots could have been fatal."

"Maybe all six together?" Kennedy ventured, but Sheila immediately shook her head.

"No, no way. Something else killed Mr. Diamante. Can I see your notes?"

Kennedy got up and crossed the space between them and handed over his notebook, then parked himself on the arm of the chair next to hers. Sheila flipped through the pages; looking for what, the detectives didn't know.

Finally, she looked up and fixed her gaze on Gray. "I need to take a look at the body."

"You need the wife's permission for that, don't you?"

"It would make my life easier, yeah."

"She was in a big hurry to bury him," Kennedy said. "She kept after the chief until he got the body released."

Sheila shrugged. "Worst case scenario, I can get a court order for the exhumation."

FORTY-THREE

"What are you talking about? We're ready to go. She confessed, for God's sake." ADA Brodie Lane was pacing back and forth in his office. Gray was sitting in a wing chair watching him.

Gray shrugged. "I'm sorry, Brodie, but Sheila Reynolds took a look at Bo's notes and found holes you could drive a truck through. She petitioned the Court to have the body exhumed."

Lane pushed a button on his phone and a woman's voice said, "Yes, Mr. Lane?"

"Did we get a notice from the Court about an exhumation?"

"We did get something from them. The

messenger just left."

"Would you bring it in here, please?"

"Right away, Mr. Lane," the secretary responded. There was a knock on the door and then a young woman walked in carrying an business-sized envelope, which she handed to Lane. She smiled and nodded at Gray, then disappeared back out the door, which she closed discreetly behind her.

Lane tore open the envelope and removed its contents. As he was reading, he started shaking his head.

"Why am I just hearing about this now? Why didn't she look into it sooner if she thought there was a problem? Jesus Christ! We just got an indictment."

"She was out of town," Henry said. "Family emergency."

Sheila had donned an apron, rubber gloves, and a facemask before she rolled out the drawer containing Big Jim Diamond's exhumed remains. Now, she peeled back the sheet. Gray wrinkled his nose at the smell, but other than that he was fine. Kennedy, though, who hadn't been through too many autopsies in his time on the force and never a disinterment, looked about five shades lighter than he had when the detectives had arrived ten minutes earlier.

Sheila glanced at him. "You okay, Brett?" Kennedy swallowed hard and gave her thumbs up. "I'm good," he lied. The ME smiled at him briefly, then turned her attention back to the body.

Someone had removed Big Jim's dark suit and white shirt and neatly folded them and placed them on a table. Although he'd been cleaned up, he was still a mess. Besides the bullet wounds themselves, there was substantial bruising and he was marked with the familiar "Y" incision from the autopsy.

Gray, especially, was taken aback. "Bo was pretty clear on the cause of death," he said. "Why did he even do an autopsy?"

"Because it's the law," Sheila replied. "To be honest, I'm surprised he bothered. He's lazy and he's sloppy."

"Then why is he still here?" Kennedy asked.

"Politics, plain and simple," Sheila said, her tone resigned.

"Well, he's been around since the Stone Age," Henry said. "I wasn't too happy to see him at the crime scene, I'll tell you that."

"Sorry," Sheila said. "Unavoidable."

"I know," Gray said hastily. "I didn't mean it like that."

Sheila winked. "I know, Henry." She turned her attention back to their victim. "There were six entry wounds, all in his upper body," Sheila said. The two in his left arm were through and through. There was some damage due to cavitation, but for the most part, those two didn't do much."

"Cavitation?" Kennedy asked.

"Yes," Sheila said. "When a bullet passes through soft tissue, it creates a cavity that can be up to thirty times the width of whatever the infiltrate is. It closes within a second after the bullet passes, but the shock waves and shearing from that cavity spread out and cause a lot of damage.

"Is that why he's bruised?"

"Yep. It's all about kinetic energy. But, since

neither of these hit near anything, they weren't your cause of death. In other words, there was nothing in the area for them to damage besides soft tissue.

"Now, let's look at the ones in the chest and abdomen." She shook her head. "Amazing, but nothing major was hit, no vital organs, not the aorta, nothing. This one," she put her finger into one of the holes and stretched the skin a little, which made Kennedy look like he was about to pass out, "cracked a rib, and this one," another finger, "clipped L4 on its way out his back. That's the one that was stuck in his chair. Serious? It depends, but most likely not. Certainly not fatal, anyway." Kennedy excused himself and went out into the hallway.

Sheila looked after him. "I'm sorry about that," she said.

Gray shrugged. "Don't worry about it. He had to get his cherry popped sooner or later," he remarked, then blushed at the crude way he'd phrased it. "Sorry," he said, embarrassed. They both turned their attention back to Big Jim.

"Okay, so that's four of the six and nothing too serious so far, all definitely survivable," Sheila continued. "He's also got this one," she pointed, "and this one. The first one is another one that hit nothing but soft tissue, in this case, what's commonly referred to as a love handle. The last one here, I thought that was probably the kill shot, and by all rights it probably should have been, but it missed everything. It passed between his stomach and spleen, then missed his left lung. It looks like it ricocheted off a rib and passed out his side. If he hadn't wound up dead anyway, I'd say he was a very lucky man."

"So, six bullet wounds and none of them cashed him in?" Gray asked. "Did he have a heart attack? Maybe from the shock of getting shot?"

"His heart wasn't in the greatest shape, but for a man of his age, it wasn't terrible. It was within normal ranges for size and weight. There was some arteriosclerosis, but that's to be expected. If I checked you right now, you'd have some signs of it yourself."

"I'd really rather you didn't," Gray said.

"You're no fun at all," Sheila joked. "Slip on a pair of gloves, will you?"

Henry walked to a rolling cart and pulled two rubber gloves out of a box. As he was slipping them on, Sheila made a sound of disgust.

"What funeral home did this again? It's on his chart, near the bottom on the left." She pointed. "The green clipboard."

Gray picked it up and looked at the paper on it. "Uh, Fleming's. Why?"

"Look at his hands," Sheila said, shaking her head. "They left him in cadaveric spasm."

"Death grip?" Gray asked. He hoped he was right; he didn't want to sound stupid in front of this particular coroner.

"Sheila looked up at him and smiled beneath her mask. "Give that man a cigar," she said. Gray had stepped back up to the table right beside her. "Help me roll him," she instructed. The two of them moved Big Jim gently onto his right side. "Hold him right there," she said as she moved to the other side of the table. She touched each exit wound gently, palpating the flesh as she studied them carefully, her nose only an inch from the still form. "I can't for the life of me.....hello?"

Gray sensed some urgency in her voice, whereas previously it had been monotone, clinical.

"Look at this, Henry," she said. When he didn't move immediately, she put her hands on the body. "I've got him. Come around to this side."

Henry rushed around the table, expecting to see something earth-shattering, but he was disappointed.

"What?" he asked. Sheila pointed to a red mark at the base of Big Jim's skull. Henry shrugged. "Okay, he had a pimple. I don't get it."

"It's not a bump, Henry," Sheila said. "It's a hole." She looked at him and saw the confusion on his face. "He was stabbed to death." She stretched the skin around the wound to make it more pronounced.

Gray squinted, then shrugged. "I've had paper cuts that looked worse than that," he said. "How could a tiny little wound like that kill someone? Especially when six bullets didn't?"

"If it hit in the right spot, in this case, the medulla oblongata, autonomic function would stop. Heart rate, breathing, everything."

"And this is in the right spot for that?"

"It's, you should pardon the expression, dead-on."

Gray shook his head. "What would make a hole that small?" he asked.

"If I had to guess," Sheila replied, "I'd say an awl or an ice pick."

"An awl or an ice pick? Who carries either one around?" Gray mused.

"I don't know about the ice pick, but a carpenter might have an awl in his tool box. Were they having any work done in the building?" Sheila asked.

"Not that I know of," Gray replied, "but I can find

out easily enough." He started to walk out of the room when something occurred to him and he turned back. "What about a screwdriver or a pen or something like that?" he asked. "Something more common?"

Sheila shook her head. "No," she said, "even a Phillips head would leave a ragged hole because the tip isn't perfectly round, and a pen or pencil would have left ink or lead residue. It's an awl or a pick, I'm sure of it."

"Could someone have hit that exact spot at random?" Gray asked.

"I suppose it's possible," she responded.

"But, not likely?" he finished for her.

She shook her head. "No, I think whoever did this knew the exact spot they had to hit to kill him.

"Thanks, Sheila. Great work, as always."

"You're entirely welcome, Henry. Sorry I had to throw a monkey wrench into your case."

"Don't be," Henry said. "The most important thing is we get it right. Maybe this will help us break it."

FORTY-FOUR

On their way back to the office, Gray looked at Kennedy. "Are you thinking what I'm thinking?"

"Maybe. Are you thinking there's a reason the spindle is missing from the office?"

"Exactly." He took out his phone and dialed.

"Morgue."

"Sheila, it's Henry."

"Well, hello there, Henry. Long time, no see. To what do I owe the pleasure?"

"Question. You know those spindle things that people use in offices?"

"You mean to put papers on so they don't get lost?"

"Yeah. Could something like that have made that hole in Big Jim's neck?"

"Yeah, definitely. Bring it in and I'll match it up."

"Well, that's gonna be a bit of a problem. We don't have it yet, but there's one missing from his office."

"Let me know as soon as you find it," Sheila said.

"I will," Gray promised, then they said their goodbyes. For the next few minutes, Gray found himself having trouble concentrating; he was distracted thinking about Sheila. I should just go ahead and ask her out, he told himself. What's the worst that could happen?

He was sitting at his desk, waiting for Kennedy to get back from a doctor's appointment, and looking through the information they had gathered when his partner walked up to him carrying a plastic evidence bag. He held it up so Gray could see it.

"Hot damn!" Gray said. "Where'd you get that?" Then he noticed that Kennedy's clothes were rumpled and dirty. "Where's this doctor's office? The landfill?"

"Funny," Kennedy said. "I had a hunch, so I went back to where they found the gun. The dumpster got picked up since the gun was recovered, but I decided to take a look around anyway. I found this behind it. I didn't find the base, but I'm pretty sure this is the spindle. It's got threads on it where it would have screwed in. It looks like it has blood on it, too."

"Let's run it over to Sheila right now."

"Tell you what," Kennedy said. "Why don't you run it over to Sheila. I'm gonna burn these clothes and take a shower before I do anything else."

"You going home?" Gray asked.

"No, I can shower here. I have three complete changes of clothes in my locker, right down to the shoes and underwear."

"Of course you do," Gray chuckled, shaking his head. "Why am I not surprised? Move your ass and you can come with me," he urged

"Nah, I'll see you when you get back," Kennedy said, giving him a knowing smile and a wink. "Say 'hi' to her for me."

Gray shook his head again. "What are we, in seventh grade?" he muttered as he walked away.

Traffic was light, so he made it to the morgue in just a couple minutes. He parked and walked up to the door and, just as he was about to ring the buzzer, two men came out. Gray grabbed the door before it shut and walked in. *Some security set-up*, he thought. As he walked down the hallway, he began to smell that familiar stench of death and chemicals. He tried to take shallow breaths and delay the inevitable, but it didn't work. His stomach turned as he pushed open the door to the autopsy room and walked in. Sheila had her back to him, but there was someone else in the room and he was facing the door.

"Henry," the man said. He sounded completely deflated.

Henry nodded. "Hello, Bo." Sheila turned around and, even though Gray couldn't see her mouth under her mask, he knew she smiled at him. He could tell by the way her eyes crinkled and brightened when she saw him.

"Hi, Henry. I was just filling Bo in on the Jim

Diamond case." Something in her voice told Gray that she wasn't enjoying having to dispute the old man's findings. She had complained many times of how Bo Shettrick's performance of his duties gave the department a black eye, but the people in charge would never do anything about it. Still, she wasn't the type to gloat or lord her expertise over anyone.

"Well, I think I have the murder weapon right here," Henry said. He held it at eye level so they could see it. He noticed that Bo didn't look at it, though; instead, he turned away. "What do you think, Bo?" he asked.

When Bo turned back to him, his face above his mask was bright red. "I think you're both crazy," he blustered. "Six gunshot wounds, that's your cause of death. So he had a little mark on his neck. Big deal. That doesn't prove a damned thing if you ask me."

"Bo," Sheila said gently, "we can talk about this later." She was trying to give him an out, but either he wouldn't take it or didn't recognize it because he continued to blather.

"This is bullshit! I've been a medical examiner for forty years and no one has ever called my work into question. I've got citations from three different mayors. You people don't know what you're talking about. I should sue you both for slander." With that, he stormed out of the room, trying to slam the door as hard as he could, but the pneumatic closer thwarted his effort at a dramatic exit.

Sheila looked at Gray, wide-eyed. "Well, that went well," she said.

"Methinks he doth protest too much," Henry said.

"Tell me about it, Shakespeare," Sheila said.

Henry handed her the evidence bag.

"It looks like blood on the spike, but it could be almost anything."

"I'll test it," Sheila said, holding the bag closer to her face to inspect it.

"I'll be back in a few," Gray said. "I'm gonna go make Bo's day even better."

"Henry." Gray looked back at her. "Don't be too hard on him, okay?"

He went out the same door Bo had left through moments before and found him in the locker room, changing. When the older man saw the detective, he launched into another tirade. Gray let him rant.

When he seemed to run out of gas, Gray asked, "You got that all out of your system now, Bo?" The older man glared at him but didn't say anything. "Good," he said, "because I want to know why you were at the scene twice on the day Jim Diamond got shot?"

In truth, Gray knew no such thing, but he couldn't dismiss the idea that the van seen near the scene might be one of the ones he had noticed parked outside the coroner's office earlier that morning. The fact that the patrol officers had seen a dark van near the crime scene was working at him like a maddening itch that he couldn't quite reach.

Bo tried to hide his surprise, but it didn't work. "What the hell are you talking about?" he demanded. "You're out of your mind." His seemingly contrived reaction told Gray he was on the right track.

Henry shook his head. "Bo, that act isn't good enough for a fourth-grade play. You know damn well what I'm talking about."

Bo pulled on his shirt and slammed the door to his locker. "Go to hell, Henry," he said and rushed out of the room.

"Fastest I've ever seen you move, Bo," Gray observed, eliciting a laugh from someone on the other side of the bank of lockers. He had assumed they were the only ones in the room and immediately regretted the remark. He went back to the autopsy room, where Sheila was just finishing up. She looked at him curiously, but didn't ask what was going on; call it 'professional courtesy'. If he wanted to tell her, he would.

"What was your take on his reaction to that spindle?" Gray asked her.

She looked at him thoughtfully. "He didn't really want to look at it. He turned his head."

"That's what I saw, too. Now, if someone walks into a room with the murder weapon, don't you think a medical examiner would want to take a look at it?"

"I wouldn't jump to conclusions, Henry. Bo is adamant that it was the gunshots that killed Jim. I'm challenging his professional opinion. That's a huge deal in our little corner of the world.."

"Try this on for size," Gray said, excitement evident in his voice. "What if there were two killers?"

Sheila gave him a strange look. "Two killers? That's a new one on me. Once you're dead, you're dead. At least that's always been my take on it." She smiled. "And I've been doing this for a lot longer than I care to say."

Gray smiled at her. "Ah, you're still a young girl," he remarked. He was so enthralled with his new theory that he didn't notice the slight blush that rose on her pretty face. "Well, a would-be killer and a killer. We know Beverly shot him but didn't kill him. What if she left thinking he was dead, but someone else finished him off with the jab in the neck?"

"Why not her? Why does there have to be a second person involved?"

"Because of the timeline," Gray explained. "That office is starting to look like Grand Central Station. Dixie Lee Wrenn shows up, then the first wife, then the second wife, then Wheeler, then Bo..." He stopped mid-sentence and stared at her, his eyes growing large.

"Now, wait a minute Henry," she protested. "Bo's sloppy, he's lazy, and he's cranky as hell. None of that makes him a killer."

"Maybe not, but I think I need to take a closer look. What if Jim wasn't dead when Wheeler was there? What if he was killed after?

"What could his angle possibly be? Come on." Looking at her, Gray suddenly realized she felt a certain fondness for Bo Shettrick, despite his obvious flaws and her frustration with him.

"Why are you defending him?" he asked finally. "I thought you couldn't stand the guy?"

Sheila sagged back against the sink and folded her arms across her chest. "It's complicated," she said, finally. "Bo has always been one to cut corners, which drives me absolutely nuts, but it got a lot worse after his wife passed."

Gray wrinkled his brow. "I didn't know he was married."

Sheila nodded. "For forty-two years. She died five years ago March."

"Forty-two years? How old is he?"

"He just turned sixty-eight. He had already put in his papers when she died. They had their retirement all planned out. In fact, they were on their way to sign the papers on an Airstream and she started feeling light-headed. She went to the doctor and he found an inoperable brain tumor that had metastasized. Two weeks later, she was gone."

"Jeez," Henry sighed. "This is all news to me."

"Bo is old-school, doesn't talk about the personal stuff." She paused. "After that, his work really tanked, but nobody had the heart to fire him, so we all started covering for him, cleaned up his messes. So, yeah, he drives me batty, but I have a soft spot for him, too." She looked at Gray imploringly. "You really think he might have been involved?"

Gray pressed his lips together. "I have to look at him," he said, although now he found himself hoping he was wrong.

FORTY-FIVE

At first, the sound blended seamlessly into the dream. Gray and his ex-wife were arguing about something that probably didn't mean much of anything, which was odd because, even when they were in the midst of the divorce, they'd seldom argued. Now, in the dream, he had started banging his hand on the kitchen table to emphasize whatever point he was trying to make. Then, with no segue whatever, he was hammering a sixteen-penny nail into the side of their house; why, he had no idea but, as is often the case in dreams, it seemed to make perfect sense. Then, all at once, the sound woke him, and he jumped, spilling his Sunday newspaper to the floor. He looked around, bleary-eyed. Here came the knocking sound again; someone was at his front door.

Gray glanced at the TV. The football game he had been watching had ended and there was a movie on, something with a lot of young, beautiful people. Not his cup of tea, as they say. He glanced around for the remote to shut it off, but he didn't see it, so he got up and made his way to the door with the movie still playing. Before he opened it –he didn't want to hear 'The Good News'- he moved the sidelight curtain slightly and peered out. But it wasn't someone selling religion; Sheila was standing on the stoop, looking as if she were debating whether she should knock again or just walk away.

Henry hurriedly pulled open the door, startling her. As he did, he realized his hair was probably sticking up in spots and he was wearing an old, stained t-shirt, but there was nothing he could do about that now.

"Sheila," he said. She looked at him; something in her expression told him this wasn't a social call and he felt a little bit of a let-down.

"I'm sorry to bother you on a Sunday, Henry," she began, but Gray immediately stepped aside so she could enter the house.

"Not at all, Sheila," he said, trying in vain to smooth his hair. "Come on in."

Whatever reason she had for being there, Sheila was a woman, and she glanced around the living room curiously.

"This is nice, Henry," she said, trying not to sound surprised and failing. "Not what I expected at all." In truth, she hadn't given all that much thought to how her colleague lived but, if pressed, she would have guessed more of a 'man cave'. The house still retained some of the cottage-style touches that she assumed his wife had provided in happier days. "Very nice," she repeated.

"Uh, thanks," Henry replied with a slight shrug, not sure what else to say. He gestured toward the couch. "Sit down. Can I get you anything? Coffee, beer, wine?"

Sheila sat on the edge of the couch and looked up at him. "Do you have anything stronger?" she asked. Now it was his turn to be surprised. He knew from the few times they'd been out socially –always in a group of people- that she wasn't much of a drinker. In fact, he couldn't recall her ever ordering anything but an occasional glass of white wine and usually she stuck with club soda. Now here she was asking for 'something stronger'.

"Um…sure," Henry said, and went to get a bottle of Scotch he had in the pantry. He got a single glass out of a cabinet. He wasn't a big Scotch drinker; the bottle had been a gift, but then he changed his mind and took down a second. He poured two short drinks. "Ice or water?" he called to his guest.

"Straight's fine," she called back.

Gray took the glasses into the living room and handed one to Sheila, who nodded her thanks and immediately took a sip. She blew out a breath and shook her head.

"Whoa," she said, her voice a bit hoarse. "Strong."

"Do you want something else?" Henry asked, but she waved her hand at him.

"No, this is just what I need. You might want to take a sip, too." Now he noticed her eyes were a bit red and watery-looking. He didn't know if it was the Dewars or if she had come in that way, but it concerned him.

"Are you okay?" he asked. "What's going on?"

Sheila held out her hand. He got up and crossed over to her and looked at what was sitting in her palm.

"What's that?" he asked.

She raised her hand higher. "When I got Big Jim's hands open, he was holding this," she said. Gray plucked the object from her hand and held it closer so he could examine it, then turned it over. There was nothing remarkable about it.

"I don't understand," he said. The object was a small American flag. Henry turned it over in his hand. It was clear it was a pin, but the shaft was broken off. "A lapel pin?"

"Yeah," Sheila nodded and took another sip of her whiskey, grimacing at the taste. "Henry, I think it belongs to Bo. If it doesn't, it's identical to his, but he hasn't been wearing it lately." She sniffed and wiped at her eyes. "And there's only one way it would wind up in Big Jim's hand."

Gray downed the rest of his drink in a single gulp. "Bo had to have been there when he died. And he was close enough for him to grab this."

"Henry...I think Bo killed him." She choked back a sob as she said this and Henry took another step toward her and put his hand on her shoulder. She immediately grabbed it with her free hand and squeezed.

They stayed like that for a minute, maybe longer, then Sheila let go of his hand and patted it. "I'm sorry," she said. "I've never gotten emotional about a case before."

"Well, considering what you just told me, it's understandable," Henry said. He stood next to her awkwardly for another thirty seconds, then went back to his chair and sat down heavily.

"This case has been nothing but twists and turns," Gray said, still making an effort to smooth his hair. "So Beverly shot Jim six times, then Bo stabbed him in the neck to finish him off?"

"Yeah, but, why? What possible reason could Bo have for doing that?" Her voice was pained.

"I don't know," Henry said, leaning back. "Did they even know each other, I wonder?"

"I don't know," Sheila said and sipped her drink. "Now what?" she asked in a small voice, but Gray didn't respond. In fact, he didn't even acknowledge her. He was staring off into space.

"Henry?" Nothing. "Henry!" She said it a little sharper this time and Gray blinked, then focused on her. "What are you thinking?"

"I'm thinking this is all starting to make sense," he said.

"How so?"

"Beverly Diamante admitted to shooting her husband, but we know now that the bullet wounds didn't kill him. And my guys saw a black or dark blue van driving away from the scene when they arrived." He didn't have to finish his thought.

Sheila covered her eyes. "This can't be happening," she moaned.

FORTY-SIX

Everyone in the room looked as if they wished they were someplace else. Gray, Kennedy, Paulson, and Assistant District Attorney Pete Peters were gathered around a table in a small courtroom. A stenographer was sitting below and to the right of the bench, overseen by a grim-faced judge.

"Mr. Shettrick, I want to tell you again that you're entitled to be represented by an attorney for this proceeding," the judge said.

Bo shook his head. "No, I want to just tell my story and be done with it. Lawyer or no, I'm going to Riverbend." Riverbend was the maximum security prison in Nashville.

"Are you certain?" the judge asked.

"Yes, I am." Gray thought he had never seen a human being who looked as tired as Bo did at that moment. "I'm ready, Your Honor," he said.

The judge looked reluctant to go along, but he blew out a big breath and nodded.

"Alright," he said finally, motioning at the prosecutor to proceed.

ADA Peters stood up and turned to face Bo, who was leaning on the defense table. "State your full name for the record, please."

"Beaufort Hank Shettrick."

"Stand up straight, Mr. Shettrick," the judge ordered. Bo complied.

"What is your occupation, Mr. Shettrick?" the prosecutor continued.

"I'm a Deputy Coroner for the State of Tennessee. I mean, I was. I *was* a Deputy Coroner." The banal, but necessary questioning continued for a couple minutes. Then they got down to business. Gray's phone vibrated and he checked it discreetly. It was Sheila, calling, he was certain, to see how it was going. After all, despite his obvious shortcomings, Bo had been her coworker for over twenty years. He let it go to voice mail. Bo was ready to tell the story of the murder of Big Jim Diamond and he wasn't leaving the courtroom to take a call.

"Do you need to take a break, Mr. Shettrick?" the judge asked. Bo had slumped a bit, but now he stood taller and shook his head.

"No, Your Honor."

"Mr. Shettrick, as a condition of your plea agreement with the District Attorney, you are required to allocute as to the details of what took place on the afternoon of June fifth as it relates to the murder of James Diamante, also known as Big Jim Diamond. In exchange, the District Attorney has taken the death penalty off the table. Do you understand?"

"Yes, your honor. I killed him."

The judge looked surprised, not at the confession, but by the abruptness of it. "Details, please, Mr. Shettrick."

"Well, I went to the office and he'd been shot six times, but he was still alive. He was in a lot of pain, but I could tell by where his wounds were that it was likely he was going to survive. Mr. Grimm had told me to clean the scene up, but he had assumed he was dead."

The judge's head snapped up and he stared at Bo, then at Peters. "Grimm? Not Neal Grimm?"

"I'm afraid so, Your Honor," Peters replied.

The judge looked back at Bo. "Attorney Neal Grimm told you to kill Mr. Diamante? An officer of this court? Why?"

"He didn't tell me at first. He thought he was already dead. He just said to find the gun and dispose of it. But, when I discovered Mr. Diamond was still alive, I called Mr. Grimm and he told me to handle it."

"And you took that to mean killing the victim?" Bo nodded. "The stenographer cannot hear you nod, Mr. Shettrick."

"I'm sorry, Your Honor. Yes, I took it to mean killing him."

"What possible reason could Mr. Grimm have for wanting this man dead?"

"Because I told him that Mr. Diamond said who shot him."

The judge glanced down at his notes. "And that person was Beverly Diamante, who's been indicted in his murder?"

Bo stood speechless for a moment, then began to shake, and, finally, to cry.

All at once, Peters spoke up. "Your Honor, we've amended the indictment against Mrs. Diamante and we're satisfied with Mr. Shettrick's statement," but the judge shook his head.

"Well, the Court isn't, Mr. Peters. We'll take a fifteen-minute recess while Mr. Shettrick composes himself and then we'll continue." But the hearing never resumed. During the break, Bo, sitting forlornly at the defense table, started massaging the left side of his chest, then his left arm, finally slipping out of his chair and to the floor. The three cops all rushed to his side and began to perform CPR but, by the time the ambulance arrived, Bo Shettrick was dead, the victim of a massive coronary.

FORTY-SEVEN

Once the dominoes started to fall, they fell fast.

After the officer filling in for Chief Wall's secretary told him what she had overheard, Gray had gone into Captain Paulson's office with Kennedy in tow. He related what the officer said and Paulson, who had worked closely with the chief, was sitting at his desk staring out the window.

"I don't believe this," he said, shaking his head. "You're talking about the Chief of D's."

"I know that," Gray said impatiently, "but it explains everything he's done since the murder."

"Like what? What does it explain, Henry?"

"Him flipping out because she was near the top of our list, him insisting it was the songwriter. For Christ's sake, he had the kid extradited from Rhode Island as soon as we went after her. What more do you need?"

"It doesn't make sense," Paulson protested. "He's the one who told you she'd be high on his list."

"Before that, he said treat her gently," Gray reminded him. "I'm telling you, I think the only reason he mentioned taking a close look at her is because McAllister, Willia, and Proctor were there and he knew how bad it sounded when he said to go easy on her."

"Shit," Paulson moaned. "I have to call the DA before we do anything."

After speaking to Paulson, the District Attorney authorized a wiretap on the chief's office phone, two listening devices in the office, and a twenty-four hour surveillance team following him everywhere he went. They also tapped Neal Grimm's office phone and pulled all the records for both of their cell phones, as well as Bo's. Their information gathering resulted in Judge King, who had issued the arrest warrant on Beverly Diamante, to issue two more; one for the chief and one for Grimm. Two detectives from the Tennessee Bureau of Investigation picked Wall up on his way into his office that afternoon and transported him to their office for questioning while Gray and Kennedy went to get Grimm. As on their previous visits, his secretary tried to keep them from seeing the attorney.

"I'm sorry, gentlemen," she said, her voice trembling, "Mr. Grimm is with a client and can't be disturbed."

"Mr. Grimm's already disturbed," Gray snapped, eliciting a gasp from the woman. "He can come out or we can go in."

The woman picked up her phone and punched in an extension. "Not now!" Grimm shouted, sounding slightly out of breath.

The two detectives exchanged a glance and Gray said, "That sounds like a medical emergency to me. What do you think?" Kennedy didn't answer, but went to the office door and tried to open it, but it was locked. Undeterred, he delivered a solid kick, just below the knob. The door, which hadn't been designed to withstand such abuse, flew inward. The detectives rushed in to find Neal Grimm, pants at his ankles and shirt torn open, in an arduous embrace with a blonde who was wearing nothing but a pair of earrings, a necklace, and spike heels. She turned, her eyes wide with shock, and the detectives found themselves face-to-face with none other than Mindy Barrish.

"You can't barge in here!" Grimm exclaimed. "What the hell do you storm troopers think you're doing?"

"Pull your pants up, you piece of crap," Gray snarled. "You're under arrest."

Grimm suddenly appeared about to faint. "What charge?" he asked weakly. His bravado had wilted as quickly as his penis, which seemed to retract into a cloud of pubic hair like a turtle retreating into his shell. To the detective's surprise, Mindy was still facing them, completely naked, and making no effort to cover herself.

"Put your clothes on, Mrs. Barrish," Kennedy ordered, "before I arrest you, too."

"Why, Detective, don't you like girls?" she replied coolly. "Besides, this is private property. What could you possibly charge me with?"

"I'll think of something," Kennedy said, and, after a pause, she complied, although somewhat reluctantly.

"Your charge is conspiracy to commit murder, Mr. Grimm," Gray said, watching the lawyer pale by degrees.

"That's ridiculous," Grimm sputtered, struggling to get his pants back up and then his belt buckled. "You have no evidence against me regarding a conspiracy."

Gray smiled, walked over to Grimm's desk, and lifted the receiver of his phone, which he waggled back and forth. "Are you sure about that?" he asked. "You need to be more careful about what you say on the phone." Grimm fell back onto the sofa right beneath an autographed eight-by-ten of former vice President Al Gore. The secretary was standing in the open doorway, taking it all in, looking both shocked and excited.

Unbeknownst to anyone in the office, another person had come into the outer office and was now standing at the door, behind the secretary.

"You son of a bitch!" the woman exclaimed as she pushed her way in, her tone a mix of shock and rage. Gray turned toward her voice and immediately recognized Neal Grimm's wife from the photo on his desk.

He leaned over to Grimm and commented, "Just not your day, huh, pal?" Grimm rolled his eyes toward him, looking every bit the condemned man.

At the TBI office, things weren't going any better

for soon-to-be-former Chief of Detectives Martin Wall. His bald pate glistened with sweat and he was breathing heavily. He had tried cajoling, bullying, and threatening, none of which worked. Now, he had burst into tears, his first outburst that didn't feel manufactured. The two agents who had executed the arrest warrant on him and were conducting the questioning looked at one another, disgusted by his performance. Although he hadn't been forthcoming to this point, he seemed to be realizing by degrees that there was no way out of the situation he was in. The agents could tell by his body language and facial expressions that it was sinking in that he was done, that his career was over and he was going to prison.

"It'll go a lot easier for you if you cooperate, Chief," one of them said.

Wall looked at him, suddenly becoming defiant. "Do you think you can bullshit me?" he asked in a raw voice. "Do you know who I am?"

"Yeah, I know who you are," the agent answered. "A perp, no different than any other perp we interview."

Wall's broad shoulders slumped and the other agent spoke up. "Look, your phone and your office were bugged, and there was a surveillance team on you. Right now, it's all on you. Do you really want to take the weight for everybody who was involved?"

Wall eyed him slyly. "If there were listening devices in my office and my phone was tapped, you know who else was involved and their level of involvement. How am I gonna take the weight?" His expression suggested he had just thrown their whole case off-kilter, but the agent smiled.

"Who says we're going to use all that? I got a call

that Grimm put it all on you, and Shettrick's dead." He leaned close to him, so close that Wall could smell his aftershave. "I don't care who goes down for it. As a matter of fact, if I had to choose only one, it would be the dirty cop every time."

Wall shook his head. "You don't understand," he protested. "You don't know…"

"I don't know what, Chief?" the man snapped. "Why don't you tell me what I don't know?"

Wall rubbed his forehead, then his eyes, and then told them how Beverly Diamante had blackmailed him.

When he was done, you could have heard a pin drop in the room. The veteran agents, men who would have thought they'd heard everything, were stunned to silence. Beverly had shot her husband six times and fled, assuming he was dead. When she called her lover, Neal Grimm, he called Bo Shettrick, who owed him his career. Years earlier, Bo had been moonlighting at a funeral home and gotten involved with a supplier who was in the market for bodies for medical schools. He was buying the bodies for one tenth of what they would cost from legitimate sources and pocketing the difference once he sold them. One night, Bo delivered a body, thinking it was that of a homeless man who wouldn't be missed. But, he had screwed up and turned over the remains of a member of one of the more prominent black families in Nashville. When they showed up at the funeral home to view their loved one, they were outraged and mortified to find a stranger in the coffin. And, since they were black and Bo was white, there was a lot of speculation about it being racially-motivated. Somehow, Neal Grimm was able to smooth things over by offering a generous settlement to the family on one condition; that they never speak of the incident. Bo was able to retrieve the proper remains –after they had been desecrated- but the family never found out about that. Once the body was prepared, there was no way to tell that several organs and both feet were missing. Now, years later, when Neal Grimm needed someone to clean up Beverly's mess, he knew just who to call.

Bo arrived at the Diamond in the Rough less than five minutes after Grimm's call. He found the gun on the floor just inside the inside office and Big Jim behind his desk with six bullet wounds in him. He slipped on a pair of latex gloves and picked up the gun, which he tucked in his pocket. As he did, he was shocked to glimpse movement from the corner of his eye. He walked closer to the victim and realized he was breathing.

"Oh, my God," he whispered. He examined him quickly and discovered that the injuries, while serious, were likely not fatal.

As he checked him, Jim had rolled his eyes toward him and said, "Beverly. Did this." His voice wasn't strong, but neither did he sound as if he were at death's doorstep. Bo didn't know what to do. Grimm had told him that Jim was dead, but here he was, not only alive, but naming his would-be killer. Bo placed a call to Grimm.

"I'm here. He's still alive," he reported.

"What?" Grimm whispered. "He can't be. She said she shot him six times."

"Someone named Beverly?" Bo asked.

"How...Did he tell you that?" He sounded on the verge of panic.

"Yeah," Bo said.

"You have to finish him," Grimm said, and Bo immediately protested.

"I can't do that, Mr. Grimm," he said.

"You listen to me," Grimm said. "You do it or I go public with your thing with the bodies."

Suddenly, Bo said, "Oh, my God, I just heard a car door."

"Do it!" Grimm insisted.

Bo stood still, paralyzed, until he heard the outer office door open and a tentative voice call out 'Hello'. He looked around for something heavy to hit Big Jim with, but there was nothing. Suddenly, his eyes fell on a large metal spindle standing on the desk. Without thinking, he grabbed it, pulled Jim forward to expose his neck, and jammed it in as far as it would go. Jim's body stiffened and slumped. Bo yanked it out and quickly crossed to a door, praying it was a closet. He pulled the door shut just as he heard someone enter the office. It sounded as if the person slipped. Then he heard a series of beeps, and a male voice say, "He's dead."

As soon as he was sure the man in the office had gone, he left quickly. Suddenly he realized he was still carrying the spindle and had the gun in his pocket. He got into his van and drove around the corner. Behind a closed restaurant, he tossed the gun into a dumpster. Then he unscrewed the base of the spindle and threw the two pieces after the gun, not realizing the metal rod hit a cardboard box and bounced out, landing on the ground.

The weapons disposed of, he drove back to the coroner's office. He had heard the sirens, but, as he passed the murder scene, he was relieved to see that the cops hadn't arrived yet. He was shaking and sweaty and his chest felt tight.

FORTY-EIGHT

At police headquarters, Neal Grimm had confessed almost immediately; so quickly, in fact, that it was almost anti-climactic. He knew they had him dead to rights. He told them about the phone call he received from Beverly, and of calling Bo Shettrick. The ADA had already lowered the charge against Beverly from murder to attempted murder. In all honesty, he knew it didn't matter; she'd still be in prison for a long time. Grimm was charged with conspiracy to commit murder for involving Bo and as an accomplice to murder for the actual killing of Big Jim. When the TBI was done with Chief Wall, he, too, would be charged with conspiracy. He was also charged with instigating the IAB witch hunt against Gray and having the pictures of the prostitute doctored to make it look like they were together.

As they sat in the interrogation room listening to Grimm make his statement, Gray realized that this was the last time he would do any of this. He wasn't sure how he felt about that.

Everyone was gone except the man the party had been for. Gray stood up and looked at the remnants of his cake. 'Cong' and 'nry' is all that remained of the blue writing on the white frosting. He looked around the room at the decorations; blue and white balloons, a giant Mylar balloon shaped like a police badge, and blown-up photos of him and each of his partners. Lonnie Bergen had driven down from Kentucky to help bid farewell to the man he considered more a son than a fellow officer.

Henry had received some retirement gifts; a gold watch from the Department, presented to him by acting Chief of Detectives Paulson, and a beautiful, handmade fly-casting rod and reel from his fellow detectives. He couldn't wait to try it out. He walked over to the photo of him and Lonnie; God, he looked impossibly young. Could that truly have been taken thirty years ago?

"Time flies when you're having fun," he said to the empty room.

"It sure does," came a familiar voice from the doorway behind him. He spun around.

"I didn't think you were going to make it," Henry said.

"It doesn't look like I did," Sheila said, lifting her chin at the last pieces of cake. Henry laughed, leaned back against one of the folding tables that had been brought in for the party, and folded his arms.

"Well, you're here now," he smiled. "That's all that matters." Sheila came over and stood in front of him.

"I'm leaving for Dallas on Tuesday," she said.

"Is that so?" Henry remarked.

"I'd love some company, if you know anyone who doesn't have to get up and go to work anymore."

Henry's smile widened. "Are you propositioning me, young lady?" Sheila stepped forward and put her arms around him. He responded by wrapping her in a bear hug.

"Well, I don't know about the young part, but I guess I am," she said, her tone perfectly matched to her sexy smile. "Is that a problem?"

"Oh, no, ma'am," Henry grinned, shaking his head. "No. That's no problem at all."

EPILOGUE

After Henry Gray's retirement, he and Sheila went to Dallas. The plan had been, once Sheila's mother didn't need her there anymore, they'd head back to Nashville, where Sheila would return to the Coroner's office and Henry would slip into retirement. While they were there, though, they developed an affinity for the city and decided to move in together and stay. They made a couple trips back to Tennessee to wrap up their lives there –Henry finally sold the house- and moved back to Dallas permanently. Henry later became the technical advisor on a handful of movies and TV series, using his detective skills and experience in his new career after leaving the force. Sheila got a job teaching Forensic Science at Southern Methodist University.

JT Wheeler married Sarah and they bought a

house outside of Nashville. JT rededicated himself to his career. Within a year, they had a daughter, Naomi, and JT scored his first Number One hit, a song called, "Baby, Why Not?" recorded by none other than Ari Fox. As of this writing, JT is still on the roster of Diamond in the Rough Publishing. Although he hasn't duplicated the success of "Baby, Why Not?" he has enjoyed a productive career. A son, Ethan James, named in honor of Big Jim Diamond, was born two years after Naomi. Due to JT's success and work ethic, he is one of the most sought-after writers in Nashville.

Dixie Lee and Rusty never reconciled.

AFTERWORD

I hope you enjoyed <u>187 MUSIC ROW</u>. Nothing is more helpful to an author than an honest review. Please consider reviewing this book on Amazon.com whether you purchased it there, received it as a gift or through BookCrossing, or borrowed it from the library. Reviews on Goodreads.com are also appreciated.

I love to hear from readers! You can find/contact me at:

www.facebook.com/rickmarchettiauthor
www.rickmarchetti.com
rick@rickmarchetti.com

Rick Marchetti
March, 2015

ABOUT THE AUTHOR

Rick Marchetti is the author of the short story collection <u>DARK GLASSES and Other Tales</u> as well as the novels <u>The River</u>, <u>Iris</u>, and <u>Murder in the Valley</u>. He resides in Smithfield, RI and, when he's not writing, he enjoys sports, gardening, and trains. He is also a Disney fanatic and was a contributor to a Disney vacation guidebook for several years.

RICK MARCHETTI

www.ingramcontent.com/pod-product-compliance
Lightning Source LLC
Chambersburg PA
CBHW071123170626
46809CB00002B/471